I0544406

Man Made Hunter

Cecilia Seiter

Published by LM Vintage Publishers, 2020.

MAN MADE HUNTER

First edition. April 8, 2020.

ISBN: 978-1950521050

Written by Cecilia Seiter.

To Kass, Thomas, and Blanca.

Chapter One

August 14, 2017

Lieutenant Omer Ağa found Professor Mustafa Şamdereli's body at 4:33 a.m., lying in mangled disarray in front of the E Blok buildings of Yıldız Technical University, unrecognizable save for the faculty badge pinned to his bloodstained shirt pocket.

Ağa took a long drag of his cigarette, letting the smoke simmer deep in his lungs. The campus, normally bustling with students crowding the busy walkways, was disturbingly quiet. Ağa felt like he had landed on an alien planet and was staring at a sleeping extraterrestrial.

He glanced at Officer Yavuz Ceylan to his right, whose eyes were threatening to bulge out of their sockets. Behind the two police officers, the janitor shifted his weight nervously and leaned on the top of his mop handle.

Ceylan finally cleared his throat and said, "It looks like he was mauled by a bear."

The janitor shifted his weight back to his right foot again and looked up at the sky, as if, somehow, a bear had fallen from it and now was prowling the grounds to claim another victim.

Ağa turned around to face him. "You said E Blok is the mechanical engineering department, correct?"

The janitor nodded swiftly. "Yes, sir, that's correct."

Ağa looked back at the body and grimaced. It was as shredded as the tobacco he rolled into his cigarettes. Ceylan was right — it did look like the professor had been mauled by an animal, and badly. Were there bears in Istanbul? The largest predators native to the area were wolves, as far as he knew. Could there be a zoo nearby?

"Ceylan, call the National Parks First Regional Directorate right away. Ask them if they've noticed any overly aggressive animals within the park - like wolves, wildcats. Sometimes you get a rogue one that ends up going on a killing spree," Ağa said. He raised a thick black eyebrow. "And call every zoo in the city to find out if anything...big...might have escaped during the night. Request backup to search the rest of the campus." He sighed, shaking his head in disbelief. In all the years of his career in the police force, he had never seen something as horrendous as what was before him. An involuntary shudder rolled its way up his spine.

"Yes, sir." Ceylan pulled out his mobile and marched down the path. The darkness swallowed him completely.

Ağa turned his attention back to the janitor, who was still clutching the top of the mop handle and staring down warily at Şamdereli's remains. He flicked the cigarette butt onto the ground and reached into his pocket for his tobacco pouch.

"Can you describe what you saw again?" Ağa licked the edge of the rolling paper and lit the cigarette.

The janitor's voice wavered as he spoke. His thin frame leaned against the mop at an angle so acute, Ağa wondered how long it would be until the handle snapped.

"This building is where all the mechatronics labs are," he said. "Professor Şamdereli...he worked in that department. I was walking down the hallway, and I noticed that the door to the last laboratory on the right was open, which is strange, since the labs in this department are locked after ten p.m. I'm the only one here with the keys at this hour." His hand slipped from the mop handle, and he stumbled forward, immediately recoiling at having taken one step closer to the gruesome scene before him.

"When I walked into that room, it was an absolute catastrophe," he continued. "Shattered glass everywhere. Some sort of sticky liquid on the floor. Window in the back smashed. And blood. A lot of blood. I knew something was wrong, so I didn't investigate any further. I called you right away. I think someone broke in through the window and carried out a massive attack." The janitor put a shaking hand back onto the mop handle. "And now...this. I feared the worst."

Ağa nodded, exhaling a big cloud of smoke. "I need to take a look at that lab. Can you let me into the building?"

The janitor nodded and turned to go. Ağa tossed the cigarette to the ground and followed. He'd let Officer Ceylan handle making calls.

"You said Professor Şamdereli worked for the mechatronics department," Ağa said, following the janitor down a dimly lit flight of stairs into the belly of the building. "There's no chance that his research had something to do with wildlife? Are there any live animals in this building?"

The janitor shook his head. "No. Professor Şamdereli was an expert in mechanical engineering. Not in the life sciences."

It made sense. Yıldız Technical University was home to one of the most esteemed mechanical engineering programs in Turkey. And Şamdereli, a tenured and well-respected professor in the department, had made headlines more than once for his groundbreaking robotics research.

Ağa furrowed his brow and sighed. It looked like Şamdereli would be making the headlines once again today.

They reached the bottom of the stairs and veered left.

The last door on the right side of the hallway was, indeed, wide open. Shards of glass littered the threshold. Ağa stepped around the janitor and entered the laboratory.

Blood was everywhere. On the tables, the floor, the crushed and crumpled computer monitors and machinery. A breeze wafted through the hole in the window, chilling the room. Blood stained the edges of the broken windowpane. Ağa's boots stuck to the linoleum with each step he took. He gritted his teeth and quietly attempted to quell the wave of fear rising in his chest. Whatever had made this mess...it was big.

"What's this room back here?" Ağa asked, peering into the far corner of the laboratory.

"What room?" the janitor called from the hallway.

"There's a door back here," Ağa replied. "Did you not see it before?" He was staring directly at a door that had been almost entirely ripped off its hinges. He could make out the faint outline of a chair in the room beyond it but couldn't see much else.

"That's just a storage closet."

Ağa ran a thick, meaty hand through his hair and exhaled sharply. "Doesn't look like it's just a closet back here, my friend. Can you come take a look?"

Hesitantly, the janitor tiptoed over the broken glass and peered into the laboratory door. He saw the door hanging limply from the frame and frowned.

"I've been in this room a thousand times. That door has always just been a closet." He paused, then said, "But I don't think I've ever opened it before."

"I'm going to need you to step back outside and against the wall," Ağa replied, removing the handgun from its holster at his hip and pointing it at the door.

The janitor nodded violently and quickly disappeared into the hallway.

Ağa advanced through the door, weapon drawn.

There was little blood in this room, much less than there was in the absolute wreckage that was the lab, but the floor was covered in that same mysterious substance — a thick, translucent green fluid that had dried and left a sticky residue. Ağa lowered his gun once he realized he was alone. He stood glued to the spot, mind racing.

The janitor was wrong.

Whoever — or whatever — had wreaked this havoc had started here, in this room. It had broken through the door, and then attacked whoever was in the main laboratory. Someone had escaped through the window, judging by the blood on the broken glass. Did they make it out alive, or was this all Şamdereli's blood?

Ağa shook his head, thoughts bouncing through his skull in turbo mode. It was painful to think at this point. How did Şamdereli's mangled remains end up on the pathway outside the building? Could his attacker have dragged him out through the window?

The wave of fear in Ağa's chest rose higher.

"Sir," Ceylan's voice came in staticky on the radio, making Ağa nearly jump out of his skin, "we have two patrols searching the rest of the grounds. We've blocked off all the entrances for the time being."

"Thank you, Ceylan. Please get forensics over here as quickly as possible." He clicked off the radio, lowering to the ground in a crouch.

The foreign green substance caking the floor smelled mildly of formaldehyde and salt. It was thickest in this area of the lab — it must have come from somewhere in this room. Ağa scanned his surroundings for the source. What on Earth had Şamdereli been hiding down here?

The chair he had noticed earlier was toppled over on its side. It had fallen on top of something, but Ağa didn't recognize the shape. Something cylindrical? Cautiously, the lieutenant stood and approached it to investigate. He lifted the chair off the ground.

Ağa felt his heart drop into the pit of his stomach and the blood drain from his face. With a trembling hand, he reached for his radio.

"Ceylan?" he said, his voice a strained, hoarse half-whisper. He didn't notice the crashing sound that echoed through the battered room as he let the chair fall back to the ground. "You need to come down here and see this."

A muffled reply breached through the static, but Ağa didn't hear it. He descended again, sitting crisscross in the sticky green fluid, staring.

"And Ceylan?" His voice sounded distant in his ears, like it was echoing in from the other side of the room. "Bring backup."

Chapter Two

August 17, 2017

Azar Şamdereli awoke to the sound of men's voices trailing upstairs from her kitchen. There were at least two, maybe more, speaking to her mother with absolutely no consideration for the volume of their conversation. She squinted against the glaring sun filtering through her bedroom window and reached out of bed to pick up her cell phone. Nine o'clock. She flopped back down onto the mattress, her long, dense waves of black hair fluttering to her sides.

Four days.

It had been four days since her father had been discovered by the police at the university, sliced into ribbons like yesterday's newspaper and left for dead in the middle of the night.

Today, at least, was getting off to a better start than the previous ones had. Her head was still pounding, as it had been since the officer had knocked on the door of their apartment on Monday morning to break the news, but at least the nausea had subsided. Azar had spent the better half of that day doubled over the white porcelain bowl in the bathroom upstairs, unable to breathe, practically turning herself inside-out, begging silently for this all to be a fever dream from which she could soon make her escape.

She closed her eyes and, for just a brief second, concentrated on bringing her mind to absolute stillness. She listened as the sounds from the street below grew louder. Her eyes stopped fluttering under their lids, and she took a deep breath in, imploring her skin to feel the warmth of the sunshine on her face, the soft, subtle embrace of the blanket on top of her.

It was a trick her father had taught her nearly ten years ago, when she was just a teenager. At sixteen years old, Azar had been easily flustered. One small setback and she would fly into a rage. She had never worked well with the idea of not having control over a situation — but this was especially true as a teenager, when it seemed like her entire life was in constant flux.

Mustafa would take Azar's hands and tell her to close her eyes. "Bring your attention to the space between your eyes," he would say, "and listen."

The world would seem to close in on Azar, every sound and scent magnified to the point where it was all she could concentrate on. She tried it now, focusing on the invisible space between her eyebrows with her eyes closed, and let the world engulf her.

Her momentary peace was shattered by the sound of her mother's footfalls as she ran up the stairs. Ediz, a small, stately woman with dangling golden earrings and kohl smudged around her green eyes, flung the bedroom door open. Her forehead was etched with worry.

"Azar, get up," she said. "The police are here, and they want to talk to you. Get dressed and come downstairs quickly." She closed the door and hurried back down to the men in the kitchen.

Azar stayed in bed for two more minutes. The thought of having to speak to another person about what had happened made her want to vomit again. She shuddered, quickly stood up, pulled on a pair of jeans, and hastily ran her fingers through her hair. She was careful not to stick her toothbrush too far back into her mouth as she brushed her teeth.

There were two police officers sitting at her kitchen table and a third standing underneath the doorway when she arrived. Each was holding a cup of tea. Ediz set a tray of *simit*, cheese, jam, and butter in between the officers. Azar recognized Officer Ceylan, the skinny tall one standing in the doorway, as the one who had come on Monday to deliver the soul-wrenching news.

"Thank you very much, Ediz *hanım*," said the stocky policeman with bushy eyebrows. Each of his ten fingers resembled a thick German sausage. His tone sounded sincere but exhausted.

"Azar, this is Lieutenant Ağa from the General Directorate of Security," Ediz said, wringing her hands on a checkered blue dish towel. "He just wanted to ask you a few questions."

"Am I...is there something wrong?" Azar developed a sinking feeling that she was being put under a microscope. "I mean...besides the obvious." She leaned against the counter and ignored the daggers her mother's eyes shot at her from across the room.

Ağa didn't react. Not a single muscle in his broad, pockmarked face seemed to move. The officer sitting next to him grabbed a *simit* from the tray and took a massive bite out of the savory, circular bread. Sesame seeds rained onto the tabletop.

"There's no reason to be worried, Azar *hanım*," Ağa said. "We've been conducting interviews with your father's colleagues this entire week. A few of them told us you were close with him and that you could possibly provide us with some more insight into his work at the university."

At this, Azar stiffened. She wasn't sure why the police would approach her after conducting interviews with her father's fellow professors. What could she possibly know that they didn't?

"I was close with him," she said, working to keep her voice from breaking, "and he did talk to me about his work, but I don't think he ever told me any classified information or anything that he wouldn't have disclosed to his colleagues."

The lines in Ağa's forehead deepened. He leaned over the table, staring over the rim of the teacup in front of him. "What kinds of things did he talk about with you?"

Azar paused. It had been a few months since she and her father had actually had a real conversation about his work, anyway. This saddened her even further. She swallowed the lump in her throat and continued.

"I - I remember he was really excited about the developments he made in search and rescue robots," she said. "He was working on fully autonomous victim detection. It was a little while ago. I don't remember the details exactly."

She could tell by the looks on the officers' faces that her answer wasn't what they had hoped to hear. Ağa continued to stare pensively across the rim of his teacup. The officer next to him took another chunk out of his *simit*. Ceylan stood with his arms across his chest and gazed at the floor. Azar wracked her brain, trying to remember if there was anything about one of her past conversations with Mustafa that stood out. Nothing occurred to her.

"He was always so excited," she stammered, "about the idea of humanity and machinery intermingling. Robots...using technology to save human lives...that, to him, was all he ever wanted." Hot tears threatened to spill out of her eyes, so she stopped talking.

Ağa still looked unimpressed. What exactly was he looking for?

Finally, the lieutenant stood up from the table and reached his hand out to the officer eating the *simit* next to him. His badge read OFFICER AHMET TOPUZ. Topuz handed him a manila folder that Azar hadn't noticed was on the table. Ağa pulled a photograph from the folder and stood next to Azar at the counter.

"This was taken at the scene of the crime the night we found him," he said, holding the image out in front of her. "Don't worry. It's not a picture of him. This was in a room we discovered in the lab that was destroyed. It seemed to have been a secret, but it's clear that there was some sort of research and development happening in that room. Do you recognize that device there, next to the chair?"

She took the photograph from him and brought it up close to her nose.

The picture showed a small, cluttered room: an overturned chair, a table pushed against the wall, broken glass on the floor. Nothing out of the ordinary in terms of destroyed laboratories.

But the object Ağa had pointed out was definitely strange, even in the world of robotics research.

It appeared to be a kind of cylindrical case. It reminded Azar of the large, impressive streetlamps that hung above the walkways in the city's historic center. This object, however, was eerily sterile, devoid of any details or beauty, and completely destroyed on one side. Its glass encasement had been completely shattered, as evidenced by the shards of glass (or was it something thicker?) strewn about the room. A strange green film coated the floor of the room.

Azar was dumbfounded.

"I've never seen this before," she said, looking up at Ağa with widened eyes, "and I never heard my father talk about something that looks like this, either."

Ediz shuffled her way in between the two and stared at the picture.

"What do you think it is?" she asked. "Are there any leads on this?"

Ağa wore a grim expression on his face.

"Yes," he said. "We have a theory." He looked over at Ceylan and Topuz, who stared back with pity in their eyes. Azar wasn't sure if it was for her or for Ağa, who seemed about ready to deliver more devastating news.

"Well? What is it?" Azar asked.

The lieutenant took a deep breath before speaking. "We have reason to believe," he said slowly, "that Mustafa was killed by something that came from inside the laboratory. Our best guess as of now is that the professor was experimenting with some kind of predator for reasons unknown. He likely kept it hidden in this...chamber. We've been trying to get his colleagues to talk to us about that possibility, but so far, they haven't given us any definite answers. That's why I wanted to come to you."

Ediz whipped her head up to look at her daughter, her green eyes big and round with anticipation. Azar wasn't sure if she could speak quite yet.

"Um," she mustered, not tearing her eyes from the picture in her hand. She was just as lost as the police officers were. Her whole life, she had known her father as the man who'd spend hours in the laboratory building robots and troubleshooting broken computer systems. What on Earth would he be doing with a wild animal?

"Did your father ever study biomimicry?" It was Ceylan who spoke this time from the other side of the room. "You know — taking the designs found in nature and implementing them into technology. I read an article about this kind of research a few days ago," he added as Ağa shot him an inquisitive stare.

Azar still couldn't quite process words, but something in her head clicked.

"No," she said, looking up from the photo in her hand, "but he did say something once about bio..."

The word was stuck halfway in her foggy, grief-laden brain. She closed her eyes and tried to focus on the center space above her nose.

"Biomechatronics." She opened her eyes again. "You know, building prosthetic limbs and stuff. Combining biology and neuroscience with robotics."

"Biomechatronics," Ağa echoed. His face softened in the subtlest sense. "Biology and...robotics."

Azar nodded. "He just told me it was another example of how robots and machinery could save human lives."

Ağa took out a pad of paper and jotted down a note. "Thank you, Azar *hanım*," he murmured. He looked up from the paper at the other two officers. "Ceylan. Topuz. I think I need to step outside to smoke. Will you join me?" He turned to Ediz and Azar. "Please excuse me. We'll be back in a moment."

Ediz nodded and ushered the officers to the door.

Azar lowered herself into a chair as the men crowded on the balcony by her front door. *Now* they were speaking in hushed tones.

It didn't make sense. Her father had been one of the most influential minds in the robotics club at the university, along with a few other professors and graduate students. Their research took them took them across the world to high-profile robotics shows in Germany, the Netherlands, and Brazil. If biology had anything to do with their work, it couldn't have come to this.

Ediz sat next to her daughter at the table, her eyes brimming with tears. "Azar," she whispered harshly, "did you have any idea that your father might have something dangerous in that laboratory?" Her tone was cold and hard as stone. "Tell me."

Azar shook her head. "I promise, I didn't know anything. He didn't tell me. We hadn't...he was so busy the last few months that I never...I never saw him." She couldn't hold her tears anymore. They spilled down her cheeks and off her chin in rivers.

Ağa stepped back into the door and halted abruptly when he realized the two women were crying at the table. "Ediz,

Azar *hanım*," he said gently. "Thank you for your time this morning. We're going back to the station now. We'll be in touch with new information as soon as we have it." He turned to close the door, then looked back towards the women. "We're doing everything we can to bring Mustafa's killer to justice," he added, bowing his head slightly, "and to bring your family peace." With that, he disappeared back down onto the street.

WITH THE LAST OF HER remaining strength, Azar finished washing the teacups and hauled herself back upstairs to bed. The headache was now pounding steadily behind her eyeballs. Ediz had rushed off to the Carrefour down the street for lamb and garlic. In the last week, she had spent more time at the supermarket than she had in the apartment. It was her own special sort of coping mechanism: carefully picking up each tomato to confirm its freshness, marveling at the radiant pink radishes, closely inspecting each and every egg in the carton for even the tiniest fracture.

Azar's ten-year-old brother, Ören, was still sleeping on the couch when she passed by the living room. He had spent every night there since Monday, drifting off to sleep thanks only to the lull of the TV playing in the background. The thin sheet he used as a blanket twisted around his tiny legs; his arm sprawled sideways to the floor.

Azar had always marveled at how completely different she and Ören looked. Her brother possessed Ediz's small stature as well as her stubborn, headstrong demeanor. Azar, on the other hand, was as tall and lanky as Mustafa had been. Her nose, long and bent slightly at the bridge, sliced down the middle of her face to the cleft chin she had always blamed her father for. It used to pain her to look in the mirror. It still did, but for different reasons now.

As a kid, Azar was always close to Mustafa's side. When he wasn't in the lab, he was bouncing her on his lap, giving her complex puzzles or computer games to solve, reading her history novels and old mythological legends. He'd quiz her math skills at the bazaar they frequented on the weekends and take her to Istanbul's various museums and cultural landmarks, letting her imagination run wild.

Once she got older, just before Ören was born, Mustafa began taking Azar with him to the university. She would sit in the back of the lecture hall, watching intently as he drew complex mechanical processes on the chalkboard and asked his students questions that they always seemed to have to ponder very deeply before being able to answer. She decided that she, too, wanted to become a teacher one day.

But in the recent months leading up to Mustafa's death, he had become more withdrawn from his family, spending long nights at the university. He seemed to grow weaker by the day — his eyes bloodshot, his skin growing pale. Azar, busy with her own schedule teaching English at the German high school in Beyoğlu, hadn't given it much thought. She resented herself for it now.

Azar took her jeans off and crawled back into bed. The nausea reared its ugly head within her gut once again. She closed her eyes and breathed deeply, letting her lungs fill until her chest felt worse than her stomach did.

There had to have been a reason his colleagues weren't giving the police the answers they were after.

She let the air explode from her lungs again. If she wanted any clues to the cause of her father's mysterious murder, she would need to take control of the situation herself.

Azar promised herself that she would visit the university tomorrow just as the nausea ripped her from her bed again. She sprinted into the bathroom and slammed the door behind her, darting her eyes to avoid her reflection rushing by in the mirror.

Chapter Three

August 17, 2017

Ahmet Mercan wiped the sweat from his brow as he squeezed himself out of the bakery's back door, overflowing trash bags in hand. Despite it being close to 9 p.m., the late summer air hung thick and hot over the city. He grunted, heaving the trash bags into the bins in the alleyway.

Ahmet was glad that the bakery was situated on a quiet, empty street. He much preferred his clientele over those who frequented the trendy, modern coffee shops in the area. They were older folks who enjoyed sitting and having a conversation with him, rather than craning their necks over their phones and taking pictures of their pastries. He remembered the time he felt lucky if three people visited in a day and how he had wished his store was on a busier street. He was grateful that he now had a solid base of returning customers to count on. He always enjoyed the slow and peaceful days with them.

The door had almost shut behind him when a massive bang erupted from outside in the alleyway. Ahmet jumped and put a hand to his heart. It must have been a motorcycle backfiring.

It happened a second time, and then a third. Ahmet frowned. His pulse began to quicken and he cleared his throat, trying to keep his muscles from freezing.

The sound was almost frantic, as if someone were trapped in a giant refrigerator and desperately knocking on the door from the inside. Unsettled by the thought, Ahmet grabbed a broom from the utility closet in the kitchen and headed back outside.

Darkness had never made Ahmet uneasy, but in this moment, he felt a chill settle into his limbs. "Is anyone there?" he called into the alleyway, raising the broom.

The alley responded with absolute silence. A single streetlight illuminated the long narrow path before him, casting long, eerie shadows on the exposed bricks.

It could have been some kids playing with fireworks at the park, or maybe there had been an accident on the main street up ahead.

Ahmet didn't have much time to think about it. He felt a thousand blades slice through his body as soon as he turned his back to the darkness.

Chapter Four

August 18, 2017

"Azar, my goodness! You're so skinny," was the first thing out of Professor Cevher Kemal's mouth as she opened the door for Mustafa Şamdereli's daughter. Azar was wearing a T-shirt that looked about three sizes too big for her. Her eyes were sunken back into her skull. "Have you been eating? Please, come in."

Azar stepped inside the professor's office, goosebumps prickling her arms as the cold blast of the air conditioning hit her skin. It had been almost a year since she had been in this room. It flooded her with memories of her father. Professor Kemal closed the door and beckoned for her to take a seat.

"I'm so sorry about everything that's happened," Professor Kemal said, reaching over to the small electric kettle on her counter and pulling a mug from the sink. "How are you holding up? Would you like some tea?"

"Yes, please." Azar hugged her arms to her body to keep warm and avoided answering the first question altogether. "Thank you for seeing me today."

"Of course, of course," the professor replied, setting on the kettle and sitting back down behind her desk. Her eyes were round and sad like a puppy's. "You have a lot going on right now. I'm here to help in whatever way I can. I can't even imagine what your poor mother must be going through right now. And little Ören."

Professor Kemal's desk was lined neatly with personal memorabilia: a trophy from a robotics competition in Berlin, a small white beanie baby that Azar wasn't quite sure how to classify, and two framed pictures of Professor Kemal's husband and her three young boys. Azar looked away.

The professor folded her hands and leaned over the desk, each finger glittering with a thick, golden ring. "Tell me, whatever you need, I'm here."

"I want to know..." The words were difficult to formulate. Azar realized she had come here to accuse the professor of hiding critical information about her father's death from the police. And from her family. There was no easy way to go about this.

"I need to know," she tried again, "if there was something in that lab my father was working on that could have been a potential threat to him."

Professor Kemal pressed her lips together and shifted her gaze downwards. The response looked almost rehearsed. Azar could tell she had been awaiting this question for a little while now. She kept her gaze firmly on the professor.

"Your father," Professor Kemal began, "was part of a biomechatronics research team here at the university."

Azar sat in silence.

"I never worked with him on that team," Professor Kemal continued, "so I don't know all the details. What I can say is that the head of the mechanical engineering department —" she rose again to turn the whirring kettle off and poured the hot water into a mug "— he had begun a new project a few months ago with them. He brought in professors from the biology department to help." She set the tea down in front of Azar and sat back down in her impressive swiveling office chair. "I'm sorry, but I'm afraid that's all I can tell you about the project."

Azar looked down at the teabag bobbing on the hot water and tried to process the information Professor Kemal had just relayed. It wasn't helpful in the slightest.

"Why can't you tell me more?" she asked, her voice crackly and stiff.

Professor Kemal sighed. "It was a highly classified project," she responded, her eyes fixing on Azar with the puppy dog look again. "I don't even know to which stage of completion they had brought it. Rumor has it that it was funded by the *Askeri İnzibat.*"

At this, Azar perked up. Her father had been working on a project funded by the national military police? That seemed out of character for him. He had dedicated his life to creating robots meant to help people, not kill them.

"Who were the biology professors on the team?" she demanded, setting the tea down and meeting Professor Kemal's gaze with ice in her eyes.

The professor sighed again. "It's unlikely they will offer you more information than I have."

"Please. I just need to know their names," Azar insisted. Despite the cold air blasting through the office, she could feel her temperature start to rise. "The university is hiding something, something that could have killed my father. I'm not going to leave this alone until I get some answers."

Professor Kemal stared long and hard at the young woman in front of her. "If they are not saying anything to the police, they are doing it for everyone's protection, not just their own," she said sternly. Then her tone softened. "Professors Müjde and Zaimoğlu. Their offices are in F Blok."

Azar stood immediately, leaving her tea untouched on the desk. "Thank you, Professor Kemal. I appreciate your time."

Professor Kemal nodded. "I hope you find what you're looking for," she said. "Your father was a rock at this university and in our department. Let me know if I can do anything else for you, Azar."

Azar didn't reply. She was already out the door before Professor Kemal could finish her sentence.

Chapter Five

August 19, 2017

Büyük Kuyu. Hasat Çiçekçilik. *Click.*
Dereboyu Cd. 15a. Rum Mezarlığı. *Click.*
Dur. *Click.*

The audio-visual processor that had been installed just days ago was actually turning out to be quite useful. Every passing sign that possessed a new word was automatically visually processed, its meaning stored in the digital athenaeum buried deep inside the robot's artificial neural pathways. Though it wasn't much use to it now, this information would likely be needed for communication purposes in the future.

It had been a long day.

Having hibernated underneath the shroud of trash bags in the bakery's dumpster the last 48 hours, the robot awoke as night fell with a fresh wave of hunger roiling its core. It didn't need to hibernate, really. That hadn't been programmed into its necessary functions. However, given the chain of events that had unfolded just a few days ago, the robot was able to compute that staying hidden, out of sight from living things, was the best way to ensure its continued survival.

What a strange sensation this was, to feel hunger.

Somehow, it felt natural, innate, and uncontrollable. And yet, the robot could calculate small hints of tension within its processing system. It was like a pair of magnets forced together by some external influence, and then repelling each other as soon as that force fell away. Back and forth, over and over. The feeling ebbed and flowed like the tides of the Aegean Sea.

Enabling its echolocation settings, the robot scanned its surroundings. By default, it used infrared technology to see, but echolocation served as a good backup to double-check that the coast was clear. The city was immensely crowded, teeming with all sorts of life forms that creeped in shallow crevices, flew in the sky, and walked up and down in the streets. It wasn't easy to stay undercover in such a densely populated area. As soon as it established that it was alone, the robot stood from all fours onto its two hind legs. Its joints whirred and locked into place as it assumed an upright position.

This was certainly a dramatic change of scenery.

Just three days ago, it had been tethered to the lifegiver, its synthetic circulatory system pulsing with vital fluid, day in and day out. Three days ago, it was a sleeping embryo locked in a basement in a university, surrounded by a group of scientists and engineers poking, prodding, testing, tweaking.

Today, it was finally on the hunt for warm blood.

Chapter Six

August 18, 2017

Lieutenant Ağa ran both hands across the sides of his head and let out a massive exhale. He wanted to lay his head down on the table and momentarily cease to exist. The sound of phones ringing and voices chattering outside seemed distant and obsolete as it reached his ears. He had never noticed how loud it could get in the police station.

The plain stucco walls in his office suddenly looked far too bare. Far too white and plain. Why had he never hung up any pictures before? Had the clock up by the ceiling always been so crooked? It was barely a quarter past eight in the morning. Life suddenly seemed to be full of questions, to which he had zero answers.

Everything that had happened in the last week was a blur. He had sincerely hoped that, after the tumultuous protests against President Ekinci that had shaken the city during the earlier summer months had died down, he would be able to get some rest. Now there was this abhorrent case to deal with.

When Ağa closed his eyes, he still saw flashes of Mustafa Şamdereli's body, sprawled out like a heap of spaghetti spilled across the pavement. He had seen his fair share of gruesome murder scenes over the course of his career, but this one was somehow far more painful to think back upon than the others.

It sent an eerie, otherworldly feeling through his gut. It seemed so unnatural for a person to be carved up like that.

Nothing made sense. A professor of robotics wound up dead in front of his university, his laboratory destroyed, with some sort of foreign chamber thing discovered among the wreckage. Forensics was running tests on that chamber at that very moment, but so far, they hadn't had much luck in discovering its purpose.

Nobody at the university who had been questioned seemed to know anything about the kinds of work that was going on in that laboratory. In fact, nobody seemed to have known there even *was* a hidden room buried deep inside the bowels of the E Blok building. Neither the zoos nor the parks in Istanbul had reported or seen any overly aggressive animals escape. Whatever had carried out the attack was still on the loose, and Ağa didn't even know where to begin his search for it.

A sharp knock on the door jolted Ağa out of his thoughts and back into reality. Officer Ceylan peered through the window, a crazed expression on his face.

"Come in," Ağa shouted. Ceylan burst through door.

"Sir," he said, "we got a call from a woman named Sezen Yalçınkaya early this morning. She works at the bakery down on Büyük Kuyu."

"Ceylan, we have a murder on our hands and you're coming to me about —"

"She found a man's body lying in the alleyway behind the building when she got in this morning. I went down with Topuz to investigate. Look."

Ceylan pulled his phone out and opened a photo. Ağa repressed the sudden urge to recoil and crawl underneath the table.

"Those are the same kinds of injuries we found on Şamdereli," Ceylan said, his words coming in quick and short, "except even worse. He was completely gutted. There was almost nothing left inside of him."

He brought the phone back up to Ağa's face so he could see, but the lieutenant waved it away.

"Were you able to identify him?"

"We have a good feeling the victim is Ahmet Mercan, the bakery owner," Ceylan responded, clicking the phone off and shoving it back into his pocket. "Forensics is running a proper test now."

"Get Sezen Yalçınkaya to the station as soon as you can," Ağa said, burying his forehead into the palms of his hands. "We need to talk to her. Now."

"Yes, sir," Ceylan quipped and ran out the door. Ağa pulled out his pouch full of tobacco and followed closely behind him.

Whatever it was that killed Şamdereli and Mercan, it was close by. Ağa let the incessant sound of telephones ringing engulf him as he stepped out into the station.

Chapter Seven

May 2, 2017

Mustafa Şamdereli descended the stairs of the F Blok engineering building and turned left. As always, he was stoic and calm, but his right hand was clenched tight into a fist. He let it go, and then squeezed it shut again with fervor.

The days at the university had gotten longer and longer, the research more tiring and more demanding as the weeks dragged on into months. Mustafa unclenched his fist again and ran it through his salt-and-pepper beard. He swung open the last door on the right with such a force that İnan, the graduate student enlisted to help work during the later shifts, jumped and let out a cry. He relaxed as soon as he saw who had startled him.

"Sorry, İnan." Mustafa mustered a little smile. "I almost ripped the door right off the hinges."

"It's okay," İnan replied with a nervous chuckle. He immediately picked up on Mustafa's somber expression. "How...how did the meeting go?"

Mustafa closed his eyes and shook his head slowly, extending his arm as if to keep İnan from approaching. "Let's not talk about that right now, İnan," he said solemnly. "I need some time to think everything over before we move forward with any work tonight."

İnan nodded and started a game of Candy Crush on his iPhone.

Mustafa sat down at the table in the farthest corner of the room. Somehow, being surrounded by the constant whir of the computers comforted him. It brought stillness back into his mind that always seemed to be disrupted by his fellow human beings.

The meeting with Professor Güvenç ran through his head over and over again. He stroked his beard pensively and furrowed his brow.

"This isn't up for discussion," the head of the department had barked at the group of professors standing before him. "We're following the protocol that was given to us. This kind of research is unprecedented and has *never* been attempted anywhere else in the world. We can't afford to let it go wrong." Güvenç was a tall, thin man with a bald head and a gray mustache. Mustafa had always thought he looked like a sullen, angry Q-tip wearing glasses.

Professor Zaimoğlu had been in agreement with Güvenç. "Judging by what we already know about this experiment, we're putting ourselves at an enormously high risk. *All* of us," she added, shooting Mustafa with a steely gaze from across the room. "Personally, I don't want to find out how this could go wrong should we decide to stray from the clear directions that have been given to us." The biology department chair was doe-like in everything but her demeanor.

Mustafa rose from his seat. "We would be putting ourselves at an enormously high risk if we did *not* stray from the task that was given to us," he argued, emphatically stretching out his arm to the biology chair. "Have we lost our minds? Where is our humanity?"

At this, Professor Müjde, a researcher in the genetics and molecular biology department, nodded. "I believe," she said, her mouth a thin, grim line across her face, "that in undertaking this project, we have already lost touch with our humanity altogether."

Zaimoğlu threw her hands in the air and shook her head. Güvenç shot an ice-cold stare at both Mustafa and Müjde.

"As I have already said," he said, his words coming dangerously slow, "this is not up for a discussion. We are following the protocol that was given to us. We have been entrusted by our government to carry out a task, and we will do so with integrity. There will be no further questions about this."

"We can always omit your name from the abstract, Professor Şamdereli," said Zaimoğlu with a smirk. "Nobody has to know you worked on a project that strayed so far from our humanity."

"Perhaps you should," said Mustafa without skipping a beat. "I think my contributions will be plenty recognizable as it is."

İNAN LET OUT ANOTHER shout, this time of victory, as he advanced onto the next level in Candy Crush. Mustafa pulled himself back to the present and sighed.

"İnan," he said. The graduate student immediately slapped his phone face down onto the table in front of him.

"Yes?" he asked, nervously tugging at his sweatshirt zipper.

"How long until we need to start the extractions?"

İnan shuffled through the messy stack of papers to his right and reached inside a manila folder for the time log.

"We still have thirty-eight minutes to go, sir," he responded vivaciously. "The centrifuges are locked and loaded."

Mustafa nodded slowly. "Good." He looked at İnan's phone lying face down, then said, "Now, let me have a go at this Candy Crush you've been playing all night."

Chapter Eight

August 18, 2017

Sezen Yalçınkaya was much younger than Ağa had anticipated.

She looked about eighteen years old, quiet and shy, her pale pink hijab enshrouding her soft, round cheeks and big brown eyes like a halo. Ağa grimaced as soon as he saw her. What would the rest of her life be like now, after having seen what she did so young?

"Thank you for coming to speak with us today, Sezen *hanım*," said Ağa as he ushered her through the station into his office. "I know it's been a troubling morning."

"It's not a problem," the girl replied. Her voice was more mature than her face looked. It sounded like it belonged to a forty-year-old woman.

"Please, have a seat."

Officers Ceylan and Topuz followed closely behind, shut the door, and sat on either side of her at the big round table. Ağa took a seat across from them and pulled out his notepad.

"What time did you get into work this morning?" he asked Sezen, licking a finger and flipping over to the next blank page in the notepad.

"Around 6:30," she replied. Her eyes, dead and distant, stared straight ahead past his left shoulder.

"Can you please describe everything that you remember happening from the moment you came in? Walk us through what you did and saw."

Sezen continued without taking her eyes from the wall in front of her. Ağa felt oddly unsettled by her offset stare.

"I came in through the front door. I turned on the espresso machine and the lights on in the cases...you know, just normal stuff. But I found it strangely quiet. I mean...usually Ahmet *bey* is already there at five in the morning, making the pastries for the day. I went to the back and didn't see him in the kitchen, and there was nothing in any of the ovens."

Ağa considered moving to his left so that she would be forced to look at him rather than past his shoulder.

"I thought maybe he would be outside," Sezen continued, "so I went to the back door. It was unlocked. The back door leads to an alleyway. He was lying in the middle of it. You saw what I saw. He was completely ripped apart. Everything inside of him was just...scooped out."

Topuz shifted his weight uncomfortably next to her and chomped into a muffin that he pulled out of his jacket pocket.

"Were there any signs that somebody may have been inside the bakery? Any sign of a struggle? Did anything look out of place?" Ağa asked.

"No, sir. Not that I noticed."

"Were you aware of anyone that might have had a prior conflict with Ahmet?" Ağa pressed on.

"No," she said again, finally focusing on Ağa. "Not that I know of."

Ağa put his pen down and sighed. It was turning out to be exactly as he had feared.

"Did you see anything else in that alleyway that looked strange to you? Anything out of the ordinary?" Ceylan asked.

"Besides my boss's dead body lying there empty in the sun like that? No. Nothing." Sezen's focus was back on the wall behind Ağa.

"We searched the area and didn't find anything either, sir," Ceylan said. "No trace of fingerprints, footprints, or tire tracks. And there was no weapon discarded anywhere either. It looks like..."

"Yes, yes, I know what it looks like," Ağa snapped. Ceylan stopped talking and leaned back in his chair.

"Sezen *hanım,* I'm sorry that you had to see what you did," Ağa said, his tone softening. "If anything else comes to mind at all that you may not have remembered before, please don't hesitate to call."

Sezen didn't move. "Oh," she said after a brief, uncomfortable silence. "Can I go now?"

"Yes." Ağa stood up and swung open the door for her. Sezen got up and shuffled through it.

"Oh. And Sezen?" Ağa called after her just as she reached the front door of the station. She looked back at him with the same deadpan expression.

"Yes, sir?"

Ağa grimaced.

"Try and stay indoors tonight, if you can."

THERE WERE NOW THREE things that Lieutenant Omer Ağa of the General Directorate of Security could be absolutely sure of.

One: Mustafa Şamdereli and Ahmet Mercan had been brutally murdered, likely by the same person or thing, just days apart from each other.

Two: Whatever had carried out these attacks was fast, strong, and virtually untraceable.

And three: He, along with the rest of the police force in Istanbul, would have to be the ones to find whatever it was and bring it down.

Chapter Nine

August 19, 2019

Officer Nasrin Demirci was just about to heat up her lunch in the microwave when she heard a loud banging on her office door.

"Come in," she barked, rolling her eyes as far as she could into the back of her head. Was it too much to ask to have one little moment of solitude during the day? There was never a dull moment at the *Askeri İnzibat*, but that also meant that she never got to eat her food alone in peace.

Officer Rahmi Jamaković stepped inside the room, his massive body nearly filling up the entire doorframe as he squeezed his way through. The two offered each other a quick solute before either of them spoke.

"Do you have everything?" Jamaković asked, looking around the room as if he had left something there and was in a hurry to get it back. "We're running out of time. We need to get moving. *Now.*"

Demirci popped open the lid to her container of leftover *Özbek pilavı* she had made for dinner last night. The savory scent of lamb, onion, and tomato filled the room to the rafters.

"Rahmi," she sighed, standing up and popping the dish into the microwave. "Please, aren't you going to let me eat something first?"

Jamaković stared at her in disbelief.

"We don't have ti —"

"We have time. Everything is in place and ready to go. The tracking systems are fully calibrated and have passed every test we've run in the last three days. There's no reason for you to come bursting into my office so worried suddenly."

"It's been five days," Jamaković replied, "and we still don't have the slightest clue of where this thing might be. Two people are dead already. We don't know when it's going to strike again."

"That's what the trackers are for," Demirci retorted. The microwave beeped.

"Why have we waited so long to find this thing and destroy it?" Jamaković demanded.

Demirci stared him down intensely. "You really didn't want to go out hunting this thing with beta tracking technology, did you?"

Jamaković looked down at his massive combat boots. "No. But either way, we need to get moving."

Demirci pursed her lips and blew on the steaming *pilavı*. "I have one call to make," she said after a long pause, "and that's to the Beşiktaş Police Station in Istanbul. Their officers have been responding to the calls. The robot has to be near this area, judging by the proximity of the two killings, but, according to the weekly reports we had been getting from the research team...it can travel fast. And far." Demirci picked up a fork and took a bite of steaming rice and tomato.

"Why are you calling the police in Beşiktaş?" Jamaković asked. "Let them run their little circles around the city while we find the thing and shut it down. We can't just let this information out to anyone, Nasrin."

"They might know something that we don't," Demirci answered, bringing another forkful of *pilavı* to her mouth and chewing thoughtfully. "They've already been on the case for five days. Any leads they might have could bring us closer to the thing before it kills again."

Jamaković shrugged. "You're right, but I still don't think it's a good idea. There's a reason this project was so highly classified. How do you think the local police would react if they knew there was a bioengineered weapon with a mind of its own running loose around their city? Imagine if all fifteen million *İstanbullus* took to the streets in a panic at once."

"We don't know that it has a mind of its own," Demirci said, shooting Jamaković a stern *don't-get-ahead-of-yourself* look. "Now is not the time to jump to conclusions. We know what we know, and the things that we don't know, we're going to find out. We will find it, capture it, and bring it back to the base. And that's all that we need to discuss right now. I'll be ready to leave here at fifteen hundred hours." She polished off the rest of the *pilavı*.

Jamaković saluted and exited as abruptly as he came.

Demirci sighed and stretched her neck from one side to the other, feeling each vertebrae crack like popcorn. Her spine shuddered as the tension released from her body.

As the highest-ranking female officer in her division, she didn't like being bothered by men constantly questioning her decisions. She gave the last word. And now that such a high-caliber case had landed on her desk, there was nothing she was going to let get in her way of solving it and proving herself worthy of her status at the *Askeri İnzibat*.

She picked up the phone and dialed the police station in Beşiktaş.

"Yes, this is Officer Nasrin Demirci. I'm calling from the national military police. May I please speak to Lieutenant Omer Ağa?" she asked the station's receptionist. The receptionist transferred her call.

A deep, husky voice picked up the line on the other end. "Ağa."

"Lieutenant," Demirci replied, kicking her feet up onto her desk and leaning back into her chair, a slow smile spreading across her face. "Officer Demirci from the *Askeri İnzibat*. I wanted to talk about those terrible murders that have been going on in your neighborhood recently."

Chapter Ten

Ediz was slicing garlic in the kitchen when she heard footsteps approaching her front door. The doorbell rang twice.

"Ören, baby, can you please answer that?" she called, her kohl-rimmed eyes staying fixated on the knife as it delicately chopped the small white vegetable into thin slices. Up, down, up, down, up, down, stop. Repeat. It was as soothing and monotonous as a metronome.

Ören didn't answer. He was glued to the TV in the living room, looking almost lifeless as he watched *Limon and Oli* cartoons flash across the screen.

"*Ören*," Ediz called again. He finally blinked and dragged himself off the couch to the front door.

A large, stocky man in a police officer's uniform was waiting outside when Ören opened up.

"Hello," the police officer said, extinguishing his cigarette on the banister of the balcony and tossing it down into the street. "I'm looking for Azar *hanım*. Is she home?"

Ören nodded wordlessly.

The police officer paused. "Ehm...may I come in?"

Ediz came rushing to the door. "Lieutenant Ağa, it's good to see you again," she said, pushing her son out of the way and stepping in front of the officer. Ören wrinkled his nose and returned to the sanctuary of the television. "Is there any news?"

Ağa stepped inside. "I think it's best if I talk to Azar about it. Is she here?"

"Azar!" Ediz bellowed up the stairs in response. "The lieutenant is here to see you!"

Ağa sat down at the table. Ediz poured him a cup of tea.

Minutes later, Azar came stomping down the stairs. Dark, sunken rings circled her eyes. Her long, thick hair, usually glossy and sleek, was matted and frizzy around the edges.

"I'm sorry to bother you on a weekend," Ağa said as Azar sat next to him at the table, "but I wanted to give you an interesting update on your father's case."

Azar rubbed her eyes and nodded vigorously. "Tell me. What's the news?"

"I got a call from the *Askeri İnzibat* this morning," he said slowly, pausing to watch Azar's face brighten as she processed what he was relaying. It looked like she had injected a double shot of espresso straight into her bloodstream.

"They called you? What did they say?" she asked, leaning over the table in his direction. "Was he working on something for them?"

Ediz brought the knife down onto the butcher block so hard it made both her daughter and the officer jump. "Azar. Let him finish."

"Sorry," she murmured, turning back towards the lieutenant with widened eyes. "Well? Was he?"

"It appears to be so," Ağa remarked grimly. "They didn't tell me that outright, but it's the only possible explanation. What they did tell me was that there is something on the loose in the city that came from the lab, as we had suspected. And, as you might have guessed, it is very dangerous. Very lethal."

Out of the corner of his eye, Ağa saw that Ören had left his spot on the couch and was peeping around the corner to eavesdrop.

"They've sent a team of their own officers into the city now to conduct a proper search," he continued, "because they have a better idea of what we're dealing with than we do here." He shook his head, irritated. "I don't know why they waited so long to contact us. We might have saved Ahmet Mercan's life had we known what we were after."

"It was a highly classified project," Azar blurted, "that's why they wouldn't give you any information. The team at the university was commissioned to carry out a secret experiment for the *Askeri İnzibat.*"

Ağa stared at her. "How do you know that?"

Azar drew in a deep breath. "I spoke to one of my father's old colleagues yesterday. Professor Cevher Kemal," she said.

Ediz turned around and gave Azar a look of utter confusion. "What? Why on Earth didn't you tell me that's what you were doing?"

"I'm sorry, *anne,*" she replied truthfully. "I didn't want to bother you or make you worry any more. I just wanted to know if maybe there was something the university wasn't telling the police."

Ediz rolled her eyes. "*Aman Allahım,* Azar," she sighed, "you need to recognize that certain things are out of your hands. Don't go trying to do the police's job for them."

Ağa looked shocked. Azar pursed her lips and glared at her mother before continuing.

"She told me the names of a few other professors who were on that team, and I tried to go talk to them, but their offices were already closed when I was there yesterday," Azar continued.

"What were their names?" Ağa flipped open the notepad and uncapped his pen with his teeth.

"Müjde and Zaimoğlu," Azar said. "I'm sorry I didn't call you right away, sir. I just thought...if they were hiding something, maybe they would sooner talk to me rather than a police officer."

"Understood," Ağa said and flipped the notepad closed again. "Thank you, Azar. That's helpful. But at this point, my first priority is keeping you and your family safe."

Ediz sat down at the table with them, the corners of her mouth running deep with canyons of worry. The kohl was smudged like clouds of black smoke below the corners of her green eyes.

"Lieutenant Ağa," she said softly, her hands clasping onto each other firmly on the tabletop, "do we need to be worried about something? Do you know what this...thing...from the lab...was? Or is?"

"Ediz *hanım*," he responded, echoing her gentle tone. "It seems we were on the right track when we initially speculated the professor was experimenting with some sort of animal. It's a highly intelligent robot that's been bioengineered with the DNA of some of Earth's greatest predators. It was still underdeveloped. It should have never escaped from the lab to begin with."

Azar felt her heart drop into her stomach. Ediz didn't move a muscle. Her knuckles were starting to turn white.

"At this point, we don't know if the robot is killing at random or if it is planning attacks on predetermined victims. We don't know what it's been programmed to do."

Ağa proceeded cautiously. He didn't want to send the family into full-blown panic. "I'm not telling you this to scare you. I'm telling you this because I want you and your family safe, and you deserve to know the truth about Mustafa's death. You've been through enough as it is. Can I trust you to keep this information confidential?"

Ediz released the death grip on her hands and grabbed onto Azar's. "I won't let anything else happen to this family," she said, her voice shaking with what sounded like a mixture of fear and rage. "We won't tell anyone, Lieutenant Ağa. We will stay safe here."

Azar could barely believe what she was hearing.

So, her father *had* been working on a project for the military police. On top of that, he had created a monster, a ruthless killing machine that was now prowling the streets of her city and ripping up innocent people who ended up at the wrong place at the wrong time. It made sense now, why the biology professors had been on the research team.

She felt the nausea creeping back up her esophagus.

"Officers from our station will be stationed outside of your apartment around the clock until the robot has been captured," Ağa said. "Because this is the first of its kind, we have no way to be sure it doesn't know where you are or of knowing what kind of memory it possesses."

"What kinds of predators?" Azar blurted out, unsure if the question was even still relevant to the conversation.

"I'm sorry, what?" Ağa's thick, bushy brow formed a bow on his forehead.

"What kinds of predators did they incorporate into this robot?"

Ediz sighed. "Azar, we really don't have to get into this right now."

"No, I think it's important," Azar snapped, staring her mother in the face until Ediz looked away uncomfortably. "If we're in potential danger, we need to know what kind of danger it could be. If we know the types of traits it possesses, we can determine how it's hunting and when. We may even be able to find out where it's hiding," she added, her mind suddenly reeling with hundreds of possibilities. What kind of animal shredded its prey to pieces like that?

"The officer that I spoke with didn't disclose that information," Ağa said bluntly. "It's not up to you to defend yourself from it. That's what the police is here for."

Azar slowly shook her head back and forth. She almost felt like laughing. Her father really *was* a genius. How on Earth had he found a way to fuse a living thing with machinery to create a monster so immensely powerful and dangerous?

"Oh, I'm going to find out," Azar said, rising from the table with a newfound river of energy that sent sparks of electricity through her entire body. "Whether it's from you, or from the professors, or whoever it is — I need to know what that thing is."

Azar ran towards the stairs. She had to get dressed. What if the robot was closing in on them as they spoke?

"Azar!" Ediz and Ağa both shouted up the stairs, but she was already out of sight.

Ediz clasped her hands together again and laid her forehead on top of her thumbs.

"Well, she is Mustafa's daughter," was all that she could think to say.

AZAR SLAMMED HER FINGERS into her laptop keyboard. Her hands were shaking so hard it took her three tries to finally type in her password correctly. She opened her Internet browser and let out a long, shaky exhale. A few Google searches should be enough to at least lead her in the right direction.

What kinds of predators would disembowel their prey and leave their bodies like empty corn husks to rot in the street? It could have been almost anything with a lust for blood. Azar hit search and scanned the screen for possibilities.

Piranhas. Crocodiles. Falcons. Even chimpanzees were known to tear other monkeys apart limb from limb before feasting.

Azar's heart began sinking, ever so slowly, into the pit of her stomach. She really had no idea what she was up against. Even if the robot *was* infused with DNA from a crocodile or piranha, how was anybody supposed to fight that off? On top of that, there was the *robot* half that to confront, too. The kinds of weaponry it could possess were probably beyond her wildest dreams. Azar wracked her brain for any hints her father could have dropped in their final conversations together. What had he always told her about the robots that he was building?

The only thing she could think of was his absolute ecstasy after the KUKA KR 1000 titan, at that point the strongest robot in the world, had been revealed.

"Azar, it has a payload capacity of 1,300 kilograms. It runs on *nine engines*," Mustafa had said excitedly to then-fourteen-year-old Azar, who was curled up on the couch reading next to him. "Do you know what that means?"

"No," she had said, peering up from her book on marine mammals and looking wide-eyed at her father.

"That means," he had said, crouching with one knee on the floor so he could face her, "it can lift the equivalent of two mid-sized cars. *Effortlessly*," he had added, spreading his arms wide like magicians do after performing a seemingly impossible trick. "Imagine how far it could throw you if it picked you up!" His hands had dived for her belly, and she had doubled up in laughter.

Azar felt the nausea bubbling in her stomach now. Had Mustafa figured out a way to create a robot that was just as strong? What if it was even stronger? After all, the KUKA titan was first invented in 2007. There had been plenty of time in between then and now for scientists to create more powerful robots.

Azar couldn't quite read the emotions stirring in her chest. She did know for certain that she was perpetually exhausted, but apart from that, she felt conflicted. Fear, anger, and despair tugged at her heartstrings to know that her father had kept such a deadly secret from her and her family. On the other hand, she was honestly impressed. And curious. She had so many questions for her father. She wished she could call him so that she could hear his explanation. Then everything would make sense again.

Azar closed the laptop shut again.

She would have to make another visit to the lab.

Chapter Eleven

June 7, 2017

Inside one of the maple trees surrounding the E Blok buildings, an owl crooned its low and haunting melody.

Mustafa Şamdereli tried not to let it bother him as he slipped down the dark, narrow walkway to the laboratory building. He knew that owls were harmless creatures — to humans, at least — but he couldn't help but remember the old Turkish superstition about the stealthy birds of prey.

"If you ever see an owl land on our roof," his mother had told him as night fell on their small house nestled high within the hills of Hayriye, "you better run."

"What? Why?" Mustafa could still remember the terror that had stricken his tiny, six-year-old heart.

"Because," said his *anne,* bringing a plate of steaming *domatesli pilav* — or had it been kouskous? — to the table and placing it before him, "if an owl lands on your roof, it means bad luck is coming. And if you ever *hear* an owl hoot, Mustafa, run even faster because that means that death is on the doorstep."

Mustafa was frozen in his chair. "Really?" he asked, incredulous.

"That's what the legends say," *Anne* responded with a hint of a smile. "But don't worry about that now. You are so fast and so strong. You can outrun him any day."

Mustafa had always bemoaned that the walkways at the university weren't lit well enough. Now especially, as he fumbled for the keyhole to the building's back door in almost pitch darkness, he wished even more for at least one working lamp to illuminate his path.

Walking down the narrow stairs had become harder over the last few weeks. Actually, doing anything that involved even mild physical activity was becoming harder.

He had lost weight. His ribs were starting to protrude slightly from the cavern of his chest, and his knees were noticeably knobbier than they had been before. His skin was slowly evolving from a tawny bronze to more of a grayish yellow. If anyone had noticed something, they hadn't said anything yet —neither his colleagues, students, nor his family. Once or twice over the last week, he had caught Ediz staring just a second too long as he passed by the mirror in the bathroom, wearing nothing but a towel at his hips. She had said nothing. Ediz never asked questions she didn't want to hear the answer to.

A rattling cough escaped his lungs as he made his way down to the basement. He turned left. The sound followed him, reverberating through the empty hallway.

He paused before opening the door on the right, leaning in slightly to hear if anyone was making noise on the other side. İnan should have been long gone by now, but he didn't want to take any chances. He opened the door just a crack and peered inside.

Empty. Every light was out. The computers hummed their soothing, mechanical notes. Relieved, Mustafa closed the door behind him. He kept the light off.

Using his iPhone as a flashlight, he maneuvered his way to the door in the back of the room. The small, silver key he used to open it with glinted slightly in the white luminescence.

The door clicked open. Mustafa turned around over his shoulder again. Just to be safe.

There was still no one there. The professor took a deep breath and stepped inside the room, closing the door gently behind him.

Outside in the maple tree, the owl screeched and lifted its wings, disappearing into the dark and unforgiving sky.

Chapter Twelve

August 19, 2017

"Nasrin, I don't think this thing is working," Jamaković hissed. He shook the device in his hand like an Etch-A-Sketch and looked at the LED screen for any sign of movement.

"Rahmi," Demirci sighed, "please don't play around with the proprietary military technology. We're after something that could kill us. Without these, we're screwed."

The two officers were standing at the still taped-off E Blok at Yıldız. The sun was just setting over the tree-lined campus, casting an unsuspecting, pink-golden glow over the palms and maples.

"Yes, but it's not —"

Demirci grabbed the tracker from Jamaković's hand with the precision of a python striking its prey. She flipped it over on its side and pushed a button. The screen flickered on with a flash.

"How did you...?"

"I told you to pay attention to the demonstration the first time," Demirci growled.

She was in no mood to play games. Just as Jamaković had suspected he would, the idiot lieutenant from the Beşiktaş police station had told the family of the deceased exactly what was on the loose. Ağa had called to inform her that he had shared the news and to request that she, too, assign officers to help protect the family. She was too proud to admit to Jamaković that he had been right about something for once. But she would have expected a fellow public servant to keep confidential information exactly that: confidential. She trusted too much in people. Demirci didn't want to babysit Jamaković *and* teach him how to use basic killer robot hunting technology on top everything else.

"It's blinking," Jamaković said. "What does that mean?"

"It means," Demirci said, closing her eyes and praying for patience to return to her once again, "that the system is syncing with the rest of the trackers online. Just wait for it to stop."

"Right."

Demirci drank in the silence and imagined sitting on the balcony of her vacation home at the Aegean Sea, cup of tea in hand, wearing nothing but a silk bathrobe and soaking in the golden sun. She decided Frank Sinatra would be playing in the background.

The tracking devices were about the general shape and size of a mini iPad tablet. They were still undergoing beta testing when the robot had claimed its first victim on Monday. The engineering team at the *Askeri İnzibat* had worked around the clock to get the trackers in shape for the hunt and finally pushed out a finished product approved for emergency use on Friday.

It was absolute madness. The trackers were never intended to be used for *hunting*, necessarily. They were designed for informational purposes, with talks of developing them as remote controllers further down the line, as testing progressed.

Unfortunately, the team hadn't had time to make that a reality yet. Luckily, the important piece of the puzzle — the tracker's ability to identify and locate the robot's lifeblood — was already in place.

A tank would have come in handy, Demirci thought. Had this not been a stealth operation, she was sure she would have had permission granted immediately to use one.

"It stopped blinking!"

Demirci was jolted from her daydream of the Aegean Sea. Jamaković beamed and held out the device in front of her. "Look. See? No more blinking."

She managed a small smile and looked down at her own tracker. Every building and walkway were outlined digitally in a GPS map on her screen. She would only see movement on the screen if the robot was close. So far, there was nothing.

"Officer Demirci, I'm presuming?"

The sunset became so brilliant that Demirci could hardly see who was walking up in front of her. "Can I help you?" she demanded as the large, stocky figure lumbered before her.

A meaty hand covered with thick black hair extended towards hers.

"Ağa," Demirci sighed. "This is my colleague, Officer Jamaković. Thank you for meeting us here." She took his hand and offered a single firm shake.

"Of course," Ağa replied, raising a bushy eyebrow and pulling a rolling paper from his pocket. He sprinkled a small bunch of tobacco into the middle of the paper's crease. Lighting the cigarette, he drew a large inhale. "What's the plan?"

Demirci handed him a tracker. "A red dot will appear once the robot has been located by this device," she said, switching the button on for him. "We have officers with these same devices in every district of the city, as far out as Silivri and Beykoz. Once it's been spotted, we have to act fast. Predators aren't used to being hunted. We need to capitalize on the element of surprise." She tapped on the massive machine gun strapped around her torso. "This baby shoots bullets strong enough to rip through nickel titanium at 2,000 rounds per minute. Don't get in her way."

"I'm sorry, shoots *what*?" Ağa felt suddenly protective over the small handgun he carried at his hip.

"The robot's outer shell is largely made of nickel titanium. It's an extremely strong and incredibly flexible metal alloy usually used in biomedical applications," Demirci said. "The Yıldız scientists found a way to strengthen the alloy using transformation hardening techniques. It's almost impossible to destroy using a conventional 25mm caliber."

"Ah, yes. Right." Ağa did not want to ask any more questions for fear of looking ridiculous in front of the razor-sharp officer. Jamaković, the giant man resembling an overgrown string bean standing next to her, didn't say anything, either.

"We don't necessarily want to destroy it," Demirci continued, "and undo all the progress the scientists made over the last few months. If we can incapacitate it without harming any of its main processing systems, that would be preferred. But if it gets aggressive and you find yourself in a life-or-death situation—" she smiled broadly at Jamaković "—then fire away."

Ağa stared at the tracker in his hand and waited for a signal. Nothing moved. The sunset was beginning to soften as dusk settled into the sky. Calls to *isha* prayer wafted from the minarets around the city. Ağa strained to listen to the beautiful, melodic tones echoing off the buildings of the university. They were so peaceful, so harmonious. It almost sounded like they were calling to him from the distance. He closed his eyes blissfully.

"Is that...is someone calling for you?" Jamaković swiveled his head back and forth, his nose wrinkling.

Ağa's eyes snapped back open.

Azar Şamdereli was running full speed ahead at the three officers, shouting his name, her black hair waving and whipping like a kite's tail in the wind behind her.

Chapter Thirteen

August 19, 2017

Something deep and primal stirred within the robot's central processing unit.

It paused, shifting all the way back onto all fours and folding its legs with a *click*. Safely hidden in the brush that lived beneath the sprawling Bosphorus Bridge, it curled up like a cat who'd found the perfect square of sunlight for an afternoon nap.

This was unusual. The sensation was something it had never once experienced before.

It was almost like a pulse of electricity, vibrating soft and steady from its center and through the rest of its limbs. It felt warm and safe, yet urgent — like a signal from another being somewhere in the distance. It was a hunger, but not a hunger for flesh or blood.

Odd.

The robot settled deeper underneath the bushes.

The sensation continued to grow.

Chapter Fourteen

August 19, 2017

"Lieutenant Ağa," Azar gasped, bending over to put her hands on her kneecaps and sucking in huge gulps of air. He was standing there, dumbstruck, next to a short, elegant woman and the tallest, skinniest man she had ever seen in her life. They were both wearing the unmistakable *Askeri İnzibat* uniforms and helmets.

"*Allah aşkına,* Azar," Ağa exclaimed, looking mortified, "what are you doing here? Did you crawl under the police line?"

The short woman from the *Askeri İnzibat* stepped forward. She had a beauty mark underneath the right side of her bottom lip, and her dark brown hair was knotted in a tight bun beneath her helmet. There was an enormous machine gun strapped to her tiny body.

"I'm sorry, who is this?" she snapped, her hawk-like eyes piercing Ağa with such a force they could have bored holes clean through him.

Azar looked at the ground, suddenly sheepish.

"This is Azar Şamdereli," the lieutenant sighed.

Upon hearing her last name, the woman flashed her steely gaze from Ağa to Azar. "What are you doing here?" she asked, taking another step forward and looking up straight into Azar's downward gaze. "I need you to go back home and stay there. It's not safe out here. Especially not for you."

"I know, I — I'm sorry," Azar said, her brown eyes directing a silent *please back me up* plea at Ağa. "I was here to speak to another professor. I just saw Lieutenant Ağa and needed to talk to him. The professor's office...it was completely empty."

Azar omitted the part of the story where she picked the lock with a paperclip and forced her way inside after nobody had answered the door. As soon as she had wrangled the lock open, she felt like an idiot. Of course nobody had opened the door. It was a Saturday. But her discovery soon proved that it had been worth the trouble of breaking and entering.

"Back up," Ağa said, throwing his cigarette butt onto the ground and stomping it out with his shoe. "Which professor?"

"Müjde," Azar replied. "She was in the biology and genetics department. Everything in that office was cleared out. And it looked like she left in a hurry. A couple of drawers were still left wide open."

"Interesting," Ağa murmured. He turned to the two officers standing next to him. "Was she a part of the research group that conducted this experiment?"

"We can't disclose any more details about the experiment. I'm sorry," the shorter officer replied bluntly. "Azar *hanım,* I'm going to ask you again to leave. We're conducting a high-risk operation and cannot put civilian lives at risk for this. Ağa will call an officer to escort you back home."

Azar was still breathing heavily, exhausted from her run up the pathway. The sight of Lieutenant Ağa had sparked a flame of adrenaline inside of her as she rounded the corner from F Blok towards the mechanical engineering department. There was still a critical piece of information missing to this puzzle, and every time she felt herself getting close, it blew away from her again like a leaf in the wind.

"I'm sorry. Yes, of course." Azar took another long, hard look at Ağa. They locked eyes. He looked almost remorseful, as if he were saying, *"I wish I could help you, but I can't."*

Ağa cleared his throat and picked his radio up from his belt.

"Um. Officer Demirci?" The towering man next to the woman finally spoke, his voice quivering.

"Please, not now, Jamaković," she snapped. Her hawk eyes were still on Azar. "We need to make sure Azar *hanım* leaves this area safely. As quickly as possible."

"Right," he said, staring down at what looked like a broad, thick iPad in his hand. "That's exactly right. So, um..." He wiped the sweat from his brow, holding the iPad out in front of her nose, hand shaking. "Look."

Demirci looked at Jamaković's screen and frowned. She looked at her own, back at Jamaković's, and then at hers again. Her eyes widened suddenly.

"What is it?" Azar felt a cold sweat break out on the back of her neck. "What do you see?" Ağa was also staring at his tablet, unable to tear his gaze from it.

Demirci lunged at Azar and grabbed her by the arm.

"Hey! What are you —"

"Listen to me," Demirci hissed into Azar's ear. "You are to obey our every order until we get this thing incapacitated. Do you understand?"

"What's happening?" Azar whispered frantically, trying not to let the panic spread across her face. "Is something wrong?"

Demirci didn't respond. "Ağa," she barked, turning back to the lieutenant, "I need you to bring Azar into the building immediately. Shut every door and window you see. I suggest you find a utility closet and hide in it as quickly as you can. Do not come out until an officer comes to get you. And *do not* go back into the laboratory," she added sternly, beads of sweat appearing under the seam of her helmet on her forehead.

"Yes, of course. Right away." Ağa finally unglued his eyes from the screen. "Azar, let's go."

Azar felt numb. She didn't need anyone to tell her what was happening. The expressions on each of the officers' faces were enough for her, but she felt rooted to the spot.

"I —" she stammered, trying to find the words as her fight or flight response kicked into high gear, "I want to see —"

"Now!" Demirci screamed. Azar jumped, amazed at how such a small human being could emit such a massive roar. "There is *no time!*"

Visibly flustered, Ağa now grabbed onto Azar's arm and attempted to drag her toward the building. She dug her heels into the concrete. "Don't! I want to see it!"

"Are you out of your mind, Azar?" Ağa's voice was boarish. His face reddened as he tugged on her arm again. "You didn't see what this thing did to your father," he bellowed so loudly that even Demirci flinched backwards. "I don't want to see you lying in shreds on the floor like I saw him!"

The cruel remark sliced through Azar's chest like a flying dagger. She felt her heart skip a beat in her ribcage, shocked into momentary stillness. Her eyes were wild with almost rabid fury. "Let go of me," she spat. "I need to see what did this to him."

Demirci and Jamaković stood with their weapons drawn, each on either side of Azar and Lieutenant Ağa.

"It's too late," Jamaković called over Ağa's head to Demirci. "It's coming in through the east at Entrance 4 already. We need them to stand their ground. They won't make it to the building."

Jamaković was right once again. Demirci closed her eyes again and summoned all the willpower within her to keep her temper under control. What was it with people today and not wanting to follow directions?

"It's seconds away from us," Ağa moaned, his toad-like face now beet red with frustration. His grip on Azar's arm threatened to cut off all her circulation. She couldn't feel anything. Adrenaline coursed through her veins, causing her breath to come in short and shallow gasps.

"Get behind us," Demirci growled. Ağa and Azar finally obeyed.

Azar couldn't see anything standing behind Jamaković. Ağa was still gripping onto her arm, though at this point, she figured it was out of sheer terror rather than brute force alone.

"Jamaković, wait for my command," she heard Demirci say. There was a loud clicking noise. Azar tried to steady her shaking fist and peered around Jamaković's gargantuan torso. She tried to gasp, but it caught in her throat.

Terror wasn't what hit her at first.

"Wow. I need to tell my dad about this," was her immediate thought at seeing the killer robot walk casually up the pathway toward her.

Chapter Fifteen

August 19, 2017

The terror came just seconds after the sadness washed away.

Azar stared on in absolute awe as the machine made its way, calm and collected, up the walkway to the group of fear-stricken humans before it.

She had never seen a killer robot in person before. But she had always imagined that if she were to, it would not look like the one that was heading straight at her. She marveled at its sleek, athletic form and structure.

Her father had done well.

The robot stood about as tall as Officer Nasrin Demirci - only a good meter and a half off the ground, its outer shell a matte white metal that seemed to fluidly stretch and bend with each step it took. It stood on two hind legs that bent backwards at the knee, like an ostrich's. Its gait was surprisingly effortless, showing no signs of rigidity or hesitation as it walked.

Its head was similarly placed and proportioned like a human being's, directly on the top of its shoulders. The front of its head was a little more flattened out than it was in the back. But what really captured Azar's curiosity was the robot's face.

It was composed entirely of eyes.

There were dozens of them. It reminded Azar of a spider - rows and rows of beady black eyes staring, twitching and twirling, analyzing its environment from every possible angle. Unlike a spider's, however, these eyes were very clearly nonorganic. Each looked like a tiny camera lens, twirling and zooming, all of their own accord. It was almost too unsettling to look at, but Azar couldn't tear her gaze away.

"Hold your fire," Demirci said under her breath to Jamaković. "Let it come closer to us."

The robot paused about five meters away and stared. Nobody moved.

Demirci was the first to speak.

"Do you understand what I'm saying?" she demanded, her gun pointed directly at the robot's eye-riddled face. One shot, and she could have blown the thing's head clean off.

Azar found the interaction strange at first. How does one begin a conversation with a highly intelligent yet highly lethal machine? Were they supposed to say hello and introduce themselves first? What if Demirci accidentally pulled the trigger too early and blew the robot's arm off? Would she be expected to apologize? Did it even matter?

The group stared in silence back at the robot. Anticipation hung thick and heavy in the air.

All that it did was tilt its head sideways. It was a jerky and unnatural movement, as if it was a puppet whose string had been pulled too fast to the side. A gentle *whir-click-click-click* sound escaped from its head as the lenses on its face started shifting. They twisted and shuddered. Some closed up while others stayed open. Still, nobody else moved. Azar realized she had been holding her breath and let out a loud, desperate exhale.

Demirci tensed up, keeping her finger tight on the trigger as she watched for a reaction from the strange, almost humanoid machine in front of them. It didn't look dangerous at all. How on Earth had it inflicted so much damage to the laboratory — and to its human victims, of course — when it looked like a man with backwards knees and a bunch of little holes in his face wearing a morph suit?

Somewhere in the distance, a streetlamp flickered on behind them. Azar hadn't even realized that night had fallen. The terror rose even higher in her chest. What would happen when they lost sight of what was in front of them?

"I said," Demirci responded slowly, "do you understand me?"

The robot returned a blank stare.

"Can you disarm yourself?" Demirci tried again.

"Demirci, what are you doing?" Jamaković whispered, turning his eyes to his colleague but keeping his face pointed straight ahead. "What happened to finding and incapacitating this thing?"

"I am not going to destroy it unless I absolutely have to," she murmured slowly in response. "We don't want to ruin all the progress that's been made in seconds. And I want to know why it suddenly just showed up here." It seemed that neither of them knew whether this robot understood Turkish, but they whispered anyway, just to make sure.

"Drop your weapons," came the tinny response from the robot's voice command center.

It sounded almost cheerful.

Jamaković's jaw nearly fell to the floor. If Demirci reacted, Azar didn't see it. She flung her head around to look at Ağa. The lieutenant looked like he had seen a ghost.

"Drop your weapons," the robot's mechanical voice chirped again. "She's in danger."

Azar and the three officers all stared, dumbfounded.

"Who is in danger?" Demirci demanded.

The lenses on the robot's face had stopped their disquieting turning a few moments ago, but they started up again, clicking and whirling in slow, deliberate circles. With absolute perfect precision, the robot raised its right arm and pointed it directly at Jamaković. He frowned and looked at Demirci. "Me?"

"Not you," Demirci said slowly, her eyes widening as she turned her head slightly to the side. "It's pointing behind you."

Ağa tightened his grip on Azar's arm. She gritted her teeth. Despite the terror overwhelming her nervous system, she forced herself to think as the robot stared her down with its creepy, twisting eyes.

So, it could detect danger. That was a no-brainer. Though Azar didn't know exactly what this robot's intended purpose was, it would definitely need to know when to get itself out of a precarious situation. What was interesting was that it could detect when *others* around it were in danger.

Why was it not concerned about anyone else in the group? Why was it lasering in on Azar alone?

"It's okay," she managed. "I'm not in danger."

This was crazy. There was an autonomous weapon that had killed her father standing in front of her, and here she was, trying to convince it that everything was okay.

"She's in danger." The robot repeated the words in the same tinny, cheerful resonance.

Demirci looked completely perplexed. Azar could only guess that her military training had *not* prepared her for this kind of situation.

"We are not going to harm her," Demirci said, locking her gaze firmly on the robot. She still had not dropped her weapon. Azar thought about how badly her triceps must be burning.

"Disengage." About six or seven of the robot's mechanical eyes spun to look straight at Ağa, who had started to turn from cherry-red to ashen white. The rest stayed locked on Azar. Ağa didn't move.

"Disengage." Azar didn't want the robot to have to tell him a third time. She wasn't ready to find out at what point it would run out of patience.

"It's telling you to let me go," Azar stammered. "It thinks you're hurting me. Let go."

Ağa blinked and released his grip on her arm.

She briefly rubbed the soreness from her muscles. "There. See? No danger," she said hesitantly, unconvinced that the robot would be satisfied.

"Drop your weapons," was the robot's response. Its eyes shifted from Ağa back to Demirci and Jamaković.

"I'm afraid I can't do that," Demirci said.

Jamaković wore an expression so grim he resembled Frankenstein's monster, his brow drooping long and low on his forehead. "Demirci. What's your plan?" he whispered through gritted teeth.

Demirci didn't answer him. She called to the robot again. "What brought you here?"

The robot took a step forward, and everybody jumped. Sweat was starting to run rivers down the back of Demirci's neck to her spine. Azar felt numb, her system overloaded on so much adrenaline that even if she were to be hit by a truck coming in at full speed, she probably wouldn't feel it.

In unison, Demirci and Jamaković mirrored the robot and took a step forward.

"Do not come any closer," Demirci ordered. "Do you understand?"

"I compute."

Azar couldn't tell if it was her imagination or if the robot actually sounded almost maniacal in its response.

"Good." Demirci's shoulder started to tremble ever so slightly, but she didn't lower her weapon. "I need you to step back and disarm."

The robot stood very still, every single one of its eyes coming to a complete stop.

Azar felt a sense of dread creeping up her throat. Why was Demirci attempting to have a conversation with something that was clearly programmed to kill? Somehow, she doubted it was going to negotiate with them.

She was right.

Before any of the officers could react, the robot lunged. It pushed Jamaković and Demirci to the side with such a force that it knocked both of them to the ground. A bullet ripped from one of the guns —Azar wasn't exactly sure which — with a massive bang. Azar yelled out and stumbled backwards. Ağa reached for the handgun at his hip and stepped in front of her, squaring his hips to the advancing machine.

He wasn't fast enough.

In one fluid, terrible motion, the robot's right arm lashed out towards him. Azar heard what sounded like a hundred swords being pulled from their sheaths in deadly chorus.

The robot had retractable claws.

Without a second thought, the claws sliced cleanly into Ağa's left arm, shredding the sleeve of his navy-blue uniform and staining it with the dark, inky red of his blood. He fell to his knees and cried out in agony, clutching his arm at the elbow as his handgun dropped to the ground next to him.

Azar barely had any time to process what she'd just witnessed. She felt herself being lifted off the ground before she could even think to scream.

Chapter Sixteen

August 19, 2017

The air underneath the Bosphorus Bridge was cool and misty, leaving dewy droplets of moisture on Azar's skin like grains of sand scattered on the ocean floor. She was shivering, both from the cold and exhaustion as her body's adrenaline levels spiked to an all-time high.

She could picture telling this story to her future grandchildren one day. If she survived. "Gather around, kids, and let me tell you about the time that Grandma was picked up and run through the city by a robot that had killed her father before committing incessant murder on innocent victims!"

As the robot had neared the bridge and descended the slope to the water, Azar was almost certain it had taken her here to drown her. Instead, it had turned and made its way underneath the giant pillar of the structure, out of sight from the shops and fish markets that lined the shore, where it had plopped her down and sat in front of her, its legs folding backwards and stacking neatly on top of each other.

Azar stared.

The robot stared back, its arachnid eyes clicking and twisting in slow, deliberate circles.

"What do you want?" she finally asked, the words almost stuttering over her trembling lips. She brought herself to a crouch and hugged her knees into her chest. Was she being held hostage?

The robot said nothing. Its eyes continued clicking and spinning like gears in a grandfather clock.

Now that they were up close and staring face-to-face, she took another long look at what was in front of her.

She could see that the robot's midsection was likely where its voice came from. What looked like a series of tiny holes was situated at the top of its trunk, similar to those of a bluetooth speaker. Towards the middle, she saw some sort of a circular depression. It looked almost like a human belly button, just a few times bigger.

It was nearly impossible to tell that the robot possessed claws when they were retracted. Up close, she saw that there were slits in its front limbs that housed the vicious blades. It reminded Azar of butterfly knives, folded neatly and pristinely, waiting patiently to rip into the next unsuspecting victim with deadly precision.

Pain squeezed her heart as she thought about Lieutenant Ağa. Could he have survived an attack like that? Judging by the extremity of her father's injuries (the police officer Ceylan had given her a detailed description of them when he came to break the news), she had a feeling that these were no ordinary steel blades. She needed to find a way to get back to the university and make sure Ağa was still alive.

"What are you?" she murmured, marveling at the robot's robust build. She could now be almost certain that it contained some sort of feline predator's DNA. A lion, perhaps? The legs bending backwards at the knee, the claws, the impeccable speed

- those seemed like dead giveaways to Azar. She wondered what other phenomenal qualities the robot could still be hiding.

"No more danger," it said suddenly. Azar nearly fell back onto her seat.

"No more danger," she repeated slowly, wondering if the robot was deliberately trying to lower her guard to make her an easier target.

Something told Azar that if the robot had wanted to kill her, it would have already. In fact, it seemed like it wanted the exact opposite to occur. She felt the muscles in her shoulders and back loosen up just a sliver.

"You are safe now." The robot's eyes, apparently satisfied with what they had focused on, had stopped spinning their slow circles.

"I — yes," Azar replied, realizing she would have to play along to make any headway with this thing. "Thank you."

The robot went still and silent again.

Azar's mind was racing, trying to find out what exactly she could say to get the answers she needed. It didn't seem to respond well to questions.

"Name," she said, attempting to make her voice sound firm. She tried to channel Officer Demirci's authoritative demeanor. Perhaps the robot responded only to commands.

Nothing.

"Tell me your name," she tried again. The robot didn't react. She sighed.

"State your mission," Azar said in the same authoritative tone.

At this, the robot came to life again, a few of its eyes on the far left side of its face beginning to churn.

"Survive," the robot quipped, its voice coming in the same cheerful, hollow tone as it had at the university.

"What do you need to survive?" Azar continued, a surge of adrenaline coursing through her bloodstream at having wrangled a response from the unforthcoming machine.

"Sunlight."

"You're solar-powered," Azar responded, shifting her weight and sitting down fully on the grass, stretching her legs out in front of her. She waited for the robot to continue, but it fell silent once again.

"That's it?" she asked. "No blood? No water? Nothing else?"

There came no response.

"Why are you killing people?" she blurted, a sudden anger threatening to boil and spill over inside of her. She was running out of patience, and it was getting colder as the night dragged on. Where were Demirci and Jamaković? They had the trackers. Why wasn't anybody coming to find her?

"I kill because I feel hunger," the robot said.

Azar was taken aback. It seemed that the machine acted on impulse, much like a living being would do, rather than responding to pre-programmed commands. "Do you know how to control your hunger? How do you feel it?"

The robot was silent again.

Azar closed her eyes and tried to focus on the spot between her eyebrows.

She realized the robot knew almost nothing of its own inception or purpose. It was like trying to ask a newborn baby why she was crying. Babies don't understand why they cry. They just understand that they have to sometimes.

Nobody was giving her answers — neither the police nor the professors. And now, not even the robot itself was going to be helpful in her pursuit for the truth.

Azar sat deep in thought, looking out across the Bosphorus Strait at the glittering lights on the other side of the water.

The bridge she was currently sitting underneath conjoined the European and Asian continents. She had always been in complete awe of the structure, its beautiful arch spanning 1,560 meters across the water, an impressive symbol of inter-global connectivity. After a group of soldiers staged an attempted military coup here last July, the bridge had been formally renamed as the July 15th Martyrs Bridge, in honor of those who had been killed while resisting the coup.

She remembered the political unrest that had rocked the city once again just a few months back, right as school had been let out for summer vacation. Anti-Ekinci protestors, led by the president's political opponent Kaan Karakuş, had marched 280 miles from Ankara to Istanbul in a brazen display of urgency for human rights, democracy, and justice. Much to Ediz's dismay, Mustafa had gone to the rally to stand in solidarity with his fellow academics and hear Karakuş speak.

"We live in a time and place where the truth has become a luxury commodity," he had told Azar on his way out the door. "Question everything and discover your own truth. Don't take anything at face value."

Azar shifted her focus back to the robot sitting in front of her.

If no one else was going to help her, she was going to have to keep digging for answers on her own. She couldn't risk having the robot found and destroyed before she learned its true purpose — and why her father had been instrumental in its creation.

"They're going to come looking for you," she told the quiet, pensive-looking machine. "We can't stay here. The police are probably on their way as we speak."

"They are hunting," the robot replied.

"Yes," Azar said cautiously, "they are. They're hunting you. We need to find a place to go that is safe and hidden. They will destroy you otherwise."

The robot cocked its head again with the same uncanny, jerky movement it exhibited earlier at the university.

Something about this odd mélange of a machine brought Azar's memory back to one of the mythology books her father had given to her as a kid. The creature that had terrified her the most in that book was the manticore: a monster of Persian descent, a hunter with the body of a lion, the tail of a scorpion, and the face of a man. The name itself was self-explanatory — manticore meant man-eater, and in some legends, the beast killed and swallowed grown adults whole, leaving not a trace behind as it disappeared back into the thicket of the jungle, waiting for its next victim to unsuspectingly stumble upon its lair.

"Let's go, manticore," Azar said, standing up slowly as not to startle it. "We need to get you out of here. Now."

Chapter Seventeen

August 20, 2017

Somebody was asking Lieutenant Ağa a question, but the voice sounded so distant that he thought the speaker was somewhere in the next room.

He opened his eyes slowly, his fuzzy vision slowly coming into focus as he squinted against the bright white lights and bare walls surrounding him. He felt heavy, like someone had cut him open and filled his body to the brim with stones. There was a window on the wall to his right. He suddenly realized he was lying down in a bed that wasn't his. The steady beeping of a heart monitor slowly registered in his consciousness. The voice in his ear became clearer.

"Lieutenant Ağa, can you hear me?" a man was asking over and over again next to him. Slowly, Ağa turned his head to the left and grimaced. It felt like someone had put his arm through a woodchipper. A woodchipper lined with thousands of barbed needles. Needles laced with rattlesnake poison.

A young, thirty-something man was crouched next to Ağa's bedside. He was eye level with the lieutenant, wearing green scrubs and a nametag that read *Dr. Ümit Gökçek*. His narrow face wore a sympathetic smile.

"That's great. Hello, Lieutenant," the doctor said upon seeing Ağa's reaction. "My name is Dr. Gökçek. How are you feeling?"

Ağa was immediately irritated by the absurdness of the question. He looked down at his left arm. It was covered in bandages from his shoulder all the way down to his wrist. The pain was getting worse and worse as he continued to regain his consciousness.

"I'm not...no," was all he could manage. "Not good. Lots of pain."

Gökçek pursed his lips and nodded. He looked like a worried preschool teacher who had just witnessed a toddler stick a crayon halfway up his nose. "If the pain is too much, I'll call in the anesthesiologist to up your dosage. Be careful. You're hooked into the IV on the other side," he said as Ağa tried to lift himself up into a seated position.

Ağa flopped back down onto the bed and sighed. His memory flooded back to him in a rush. How long had he been unconscious for? Where was Azar? Was she okay? Had they found the robot yet? He needed his arm back in working condition, and he needed to get out of the hospital right away. Where were Demirci and Jamaković?

The doctor partially answered that question for him.

"A colleague of yours is outside. He came to check in on you and see how you're doing. Is it OK if I let him in?" Dr. Gökçek asked.

"Yes, please bring him in," Ağa gasped, a fresh wave of stinging pain shooting up his left arm. "And the anesthesiologist too. Bring them as fast as possible."

Dr. Gökçek smiled again and got up to open the door. Out of the corner of his eye, Ağa saw a giant figure bend down to step through the doorway and into the room. Jamaković lumbered over to Ağa's bedside and kneeled just like Dr. Gökçek had. The doctor left the room silently and closed the door behind him.

"Jamaković," Ağa hissed. "What time is it? Did they catch it? Where is Azar, is she safe?"

"Easy, Lieutenant," Jamaković said, giving him an uneasy, sideways stare. "Don't get yourself too worked up."

Ağa realized that the beeping of the heart monitor had sharply quickened its pace.

"It's been about fifteen hours since you were brought here," Jamaković said. "It's almost twelve-thirty on Sunday."

"Where's Azar?" Ağa couldn't believe he had been out for so long. Fifteen hours were far too many to be unconscious for. He dreaded hearing Jamaković's answer.

"We...we don't know," the military officer admitted, standing up to pull over a chair from the corner of the room and plopping his behemoth body into its tiny frame.

"What?" Ağa snapped. "Do you know if she's alive? What happened?" With every question he spat, his volume increased.

"Easy," Jamaković repeated, sternly this time. "Demirci and the rest of the military police are on it. After it attacked you, it picked her up and fled. It's incredibly fast, Omer *bey*. We couldn't shoot at it without risk of hitting Azar in the process."

"So, it's gone? Have you been able to locate it with your tracking devices?"

"We chased it down as far as we could and know that it took her in the direction of the strait. But as we unfortunately discovered yesterday for the first time..." Jamaković put a hand to his forehead. "The trackers can't detect the robot once it's out of a certain radius. It needs to be within eight kilometers of us to be able to detect it. This technology is still severely underdeveloped."

Despite the searing pain coursing up his arm, Ağa felt like laughing. An eight-kilometer radius to detect something that could travel at ninety miles per hour on two feet? This had to be some sort of cruel joke.

"Demirci led the search party down to the water, but so far, we've had no luck detecting where it could have taken her. We haven't found a body, either. So, we're still hopeful."

Ağa relaxed just a little bit upon hearing this. He knew he would be sick if he saw Azar's body in the same mangled disarray that her father's had been in.

There was a gentle knock on the door. Dr. Gökçek stepped back inside, accompanied by a woman with springy, curly hair wearing glasses and a white lab coat.

"Hi, Lieutenant Ağa," the woman said, approaching his bedside. "I'm glad that you're up and able to talk. That must have been quite a scare, getting sliced up by the helicopter like that!" She reached for the IV fluid and cranked a dial on a gray box standing on a table next to Ağa's bed.

Ağa shot a wary glance at Jamaković, who returned it with an intense *play along with this or I'll rip the painkillers right out of your blood vessels* stare. Ağa blinked. He saw now why Demirci seemed to be the commanding officer of the two.

"Yes," he said slowly, trying to keep his face from showing any hints of surprise. "Quite the scare."

The anesthesiologist took a step back and scribbled something down on the clipboard that was hanging off the foot of Ağa's bed. A few seconds later, he could feel the pain in his arm begin to quell. He sighed and settled deeper into the bed, a sudden exhaustion overcoming his entire body.

"Does that feel better?" she asked with a small smile, putting the clipboard back.

"Yes. Very much so. Thank you," Ağa said genuinely. He turned to Dr. Gökçek. "How much longer do I need to be here? How is my arm looking?"

"You got very lucky," the doctor responded, seriousness seeping into his tone. "You sustained extremely deep cuts to your tricep and forearm, which almost destroyed your brachial artery and median nerve. You lost a lot of blood. We patched you up together nicely, but it's going to be a few weeks before you can use your arm like you used to. We'd recommend scheduling follow-up appointments for physical therapy to ensure it heals like normal."

"What?" Ağa cried, incredulous. "Weeks? I don't have weeks. I need it today." Jamaković gave him an anguished, pitiful look.

"I'm sorry, Lieutenant," the doctor replied, the same close-lipped, worried-preschool-teacher smile spreading across his face. "I know the work you do is important, but we want to ensure that you heal properly so this injury doesn't impede your work in the future."

"I understand," Ağa said grimly. "Thank you."

Dr. Gökçek gave a quick nod. "I'll leave you two to it." He stepped back out of the room with the anesthesiologist.

Ağa gave Jamaković a hard stare-down. The officer shifted nervously in his seat.

"Rahmi *bey*. I need you to get me out of here," Ağa said, gritting his teeth as he ripped the IV drip from his veins.

Chapter Eighteen

August 20, 2017

When Azar woke up, dawn was approaching, casting a brilliant glow on the surface of the Bosphorus Strait. It looked like someone had thrown a string of fluorescent orange jewels into the water, where they were now breaking apart and floating peacefully through the currents.

She sat up, her back and sides stiff from spending the night on a cold, hard stone floor. She stood and stretched, leaning her head from side to side in an attempt to crack the soreness from her neck.

The robot stared from the corner of the room, its eyes gently whirring as they spun their incessant circles around its flattened face.

"Good morning," she said sleepily. It felt oddly inappropriate to say that to a machine, but it would have felt weird saying nothing at all, too.

The night had been a long one.

After the perilous journey across the Bosphorus Bridge over to Istanbul's Üsküdar district on the Asian continent, Azar questioned all the decisions she had made over the last twenty-four hours with great deliberation.

The robot had picked her up and run, just as it had when it plucked her from the university and brought her to the bridge.

This time, though, it had run much faster, and Azar had feared the winds would rip the skin right off her face as they raced past cars and buses, their headlights becoming streams of yellow in Azar's blurred, teary vision. It hadn't been a long commute, and under the cover of darkness and lightning speed, Azar hadn't been worried about being seen. But this method of travel gave her an uneasy feeling, as if she had lost a sense of control over her own mobility. The prospect terrified her, but she had realized she had no other choice than to grit her teeth and trust the process in this situation. Still, she feared she would become wholly at the mercy of the manticore.

The word suited the robot nicely. The more she stared at it and its clicking, twirling eyes, the better it sounded in her head.

In typical fashion, the robot didn't respond to her morning greeting.

The first thing Azar had noticed upon reaching Üsküdar was the massive palace, immediately to the north of the bridge. Azar had been to *Beylerbeyi Sarayı* only once before, on a school field trip in third grade. It was a beautiful, sprawling building, built as a summer residence during Ottoman rule in the 1860s. Grandiose arches and pillars swept across the face of the palace, which was surrounded by elegant lamp posts that reminded Azar more of Rodin sculptures than public utilities. Stout, stately palms stood at the building's four corners. A few outlook posts, resembling miniature, domed palaces themselves, peppered the wall that surrounded the perimeter of the grounds.

"Go left," Azar had commanded when she could speak again, tears streaming across her cheekbones from the wind. She didn't have a concrete plan, but she knew that hiding in plain sight was sometimes the best way to stay under the radar. Who would think to check a historic building like this for a runaway robot? There would be nobody in the palace this late either, making it an easy pit stop for the night. And she'd had a feeling that, somehow, the robot would be able to get them into the building with no problem. Somewhat emboldened after picking the lock of Professor Müjde's office door, Azar hadn't been bothered by the prospect of breaking into a historic monument with a dangerous autonomous weapon and staying the night.

Her feeling had been correct. The robot had ripped one of the palace's back doors clean off its hinges and waltzed right in. It had located and deactivated the beeping alarm system in two minutes flat. Free to wander the palace, the unlikely duo had found a staircase leading to the cold, dark basement of the building. Azar had reasoned it was safer there than upstairs, where they might be spotted through a window.

Now, sitting on the freezing stones of the palace floor at barely six in the morning, shivering from cold and anticipation, the absolute insanity of her situation began to sink in. She wondered if her father would have been proud of her for boldly embarking on a highly dangerous—and now highly illegal—quest for the truth. Perhaps he would have just put his palm to his forehead and sighed.

"Do you understand the word manticore?" Azar asked.

"Manti-core," the robot repeated. It broke the word in two as its audio processing unit stored the new word in its digital athenaeum.

Azar found this almost endearing. "Yes," she said. "It means man-eater. It's a mythological mix between a lion, a man, and a scorpion."

The robot was silent.

"I think you might have been built with the manticore in mind." Azar sighed. "I think that's what I'll call you from now on. What did you just say? Manti-core. Manti for short."

Azar felt foolish, but if she was to establish some sort of trust between the robot and herself, she at least needed a name to address it by.

Manti's eyes slowed their circling and came to a halt.

"What can you see?" she asked, genuinely curious about the perplexing anatomy of this mysterious machine.

Manti stared straight ahead and then said, "The visual processors allow me to scan my surroundings using infrared technology. I can see in front, behind, and to the sides," it chirped. "I am also able to activate an echolocation system within my audio-visual processor to discover things I cannot see in my environment."

"That's fascinating," she said, a triumphant wave of joy ripple through her chest. The robot was finally beginning to show signs of cooperation. Perhaps giving it a name actually had locked in a layer of trust between the two. She pressed on, itching for more insight into its origin story.

"Where did you come from?" Azar sat down in front of Manti, legs crisscross on the floor.

"The lifegiver," Manti said. Some of its eyes started to twist again.

"The lifegiver?" Azar scooted in a little closer. "Can you tell me more? Who is the lifegiver?" Could Manti have been talking about her father?

"The lifegiver," Manti repeated. "It gave me life for many, many months, until I was strong enough to break free."

Azar could feel the hairs on the back of her neck start to prickle. Despite feeling the chilly basement air on her bare arms, she sensed her body temperature rising. Her heart fluttered like a caged hummingbird in her chest.

"It...it fed you?" she asked, her mind rushing to put together the pieces from the past week's conversations. Her eyes landed on the circular depression on Manti's midsection.

Despite the headway she felt she was making with the robot, fear lingered on within her. She had embarked on this ridiculous journey in hopes of wrangling some information on the robot, its purpose, and her father's death. What happened once she found out that information? Worse — what if she *never* found those things out?

Suddenly, Manti perked up, rising swiftly onto two legs with a *click* of its joints. Its eyes began to spin more and more frantically.

"Do you see something?" Azar stood up too, her arms tingling as goosebumps appeared on her flesh.

"No," Manti responded. "I hear it. There is someone in this building. We need to go."

Without another word, the robot scooped Azar back into its arms and ran.

Chapter Nineteen

August 20, 2017

Azar could barely hear the incoherent shouts coming from the palace's upper parlor as she and Manti ripped through the back door and onto the lawn.

Shit. She squeezed her eyes shut. There was nowhere to hide in the sprawling imperial garden. Their best bet was taking to the building's perimeter, hiding in the space between the wall and the water. If no one saw them get there, no one would think to look.

"Go to the water," she gasped. "We can hide behind the wall."

Manti didn't argue. It expertly switched course to the south, dropping Azar in front of the wall as soon as they reached it.

The wall was more of a ledge, reaching up only to about her hip. Azar scrambled over it and lay on her back, flattening her body on the narrow strip of asphalt that lay before the water. Manti copied her every move, sinking onto all fours and becoming a large, compact rectangle at her head. She closed her eyes again and tried to steady her breath, ignoring the pain of the asphalt floor pushing against her spine. She felt a twinge of fear with Manti being so close to her face, but she swallowed it down and tried to breathe.

"Did anyone see us?" she asked, panting.

"There is nobody outside the building," Manti responded, eyes twisting. "They are still inside."

Azar became suddenly panicked that she may soon witness a bloodbath should the robot become aggressive in its defense.

"Do not hurt anyone," she whispered. "Okay? Listen to me. None of that ripping people open thing right now. If you do that again, it will put us in even more danger than we're already in."

Manti's eyes twirled and twirled, but the robot didn't say anything.

There were no gaps or holes in the wall, so Azar couldn't see if anyone was approaching. She looked out at the water and at the sprawling bridge in front of her. A few cars had started their commute across the strait, but the city was still relatively quiet this early in the morning. She wracked her brain, trying to think of their next move.

Could Manti swim?

She brushed the thought away as soon as it came. There was no way she was stepping foot into the water and then running in sopping wet clothes. There had to be another way out.

Manti's eyes were still twisting on its head when the robot's voice quipped, "We should go southeast. There is relatively little activity that I can sense in that direction."

Azar nodded, sitting up slowly to a crouch. "Can we go now? We need to leave this area as soon as possible."

Manti paused, then said, "Yes."

The robot picked her up and carried her into the distance once again.

LIEUTENANT AĞA HAD just stepped back into his office at the Beşiktaş Police Station, thoughts swarming amid the ever-ringing telephones and chatter, when Officer Ceylan nearly body-slammed into him from the right.

Ağa cried out, startled, cradling his bandaged arm to his chest. The morphine had pretty much completely left his body, and he was starting to mildly regret his decision to have Officer Jamaković jailbreak him from the hospital.

"Lieutenant!" Ceylan exclaimed. "I'm sorry, I—what? What happened to your arm?" The young officer's voice turned from excitement to worry as his eyes landed on Ağa's left side.

"It's a long story, Ceylan," Ağa grumbled, pushing open the door to his office. He glanced at the clock near the ceiling. 2:15.

He needed a moment alone to think. His ride back to the station from the hospital played over again in his head.

His escape from Acıbadem Fulya Hospital had not gone according to plan. Ağa had implored the military officer to bring him to where Demirci had continued the search, but his hopes had been quickly quashed when Demirci radioed into Jamaković's walkie talkie.

"RAHMI, do you copy?" came the officer's staticky voice. "I'm at the waterfront. What's the update?"

"Um," had been Jamaković's reply. Ağa shot him a silent plea for silence. Despite the direness of the situation, neither was ready to admit to Demirci that they had broken Ağa out of the hospital without clearance. "Lieutenant Ağa is still in the hospital. He's woken up from surgery but will need a few more days to recover."

"Good," Demirci's crackly voice said through the radio. "I'm glad he's doing alright. It's probably best to have him out of the way right now, anyway."

Jamaković let out a nervous laugh. Ağa furrowed his brow and looked out of the window at the passing trees and buildings.

"Listen, Rahmi..." came Demirci again. "Are you on your way back from the hospital now? I need you to meet me at the Abdullahağa roundabout as soon as possible. We've lost it again. I think we're underestimating the complexity of this robot. We need to put ourselves in its position, start putting ourselves in its shoes. I mean, a military weapon with biologically engineered killing instincts, intended for riot control and sting operations. Where would it be? And why is it killing randomly, without provocation? You'd think something like this would be hunting a certain demographic, or perhaps crowds, but it's not behaving in a controlled pattern."

Upon hearing this, Ağa turned back to Jamaković, his eyes wide. Riot control and sting operations? He suddenly became very aware that he was intruding in on a conversation he was never supposed to hear.

Jamaković was clearly flustered, attempting to stay in control of both the vehicle and his voice, which was threatening to crack at any instant. Ağa fought back a chuckle. Somehow, he'd always known that Jamaković wasn't the kind of person who was able to multitask.

"Ah, yes..." was all Jamaković could muster as he hit the gas and cranked the steering wheel to the right. The car lurched, leaning dangerously over on its side. Ağa clenched his teeth in agony as the pain bulleted from his shoulder down to his wrist again. He tried to remain silent.

"Anyway. Just think about it while you're driving. We'll talk more when you get here," Demirci said. "Over." The radio went silent.

Jamaković's face had turned to stone. He turned to the lieutenant. "What did you hear?" he asked shrilly.

"What do you mean what did I hear?" Ağa cried, a fresh batch of rage starting to boil in his chest. "I'm right next to you! I heard everything!"

Jamaković slammed on the brakes. The car screeched to a halt at a stoplight. A group of schoolchildren, no older than eight or nine years old, was crossing the street, following their teacher like a family of ducklings waddling after their mother.

"No," Jamaković growled. "You heard nothing. Do you understand me? Nothing at all."

Ağa suddenly felt more afraid of the oafish officer sitting to his left than he ever thought he would in his life. The silence between them hung thick and heavy, uncomfortable like the humidity in the air right before a massive thunderstorm.

"I understand," Ağa mumbled, turning his head to look back out of the window again. They were rounding the corner to the police station.

"See to it that we don't find you near the robot or Azar Şamdereli again," Jamaković said, leaning over and popping open the passenger door.

AĞA NOW STOOD ABOVE his desk, staring at the mess of manila folders and crumpled papers he had ripped from his notepad, the pain in his arm growing stronger by the second.

So, the military police had commissioned the researchers to create a lethal robot for use in riot control.

His mind flashed to the protests that had taken the city by storm just months ago. Lieutenant Ağa was not a riot officer and, therefore, hadn't taken part in the actual crackdown on protestors. He had been stationed largely at the protest led by Ekinci's opposition, employed to keep the marchers safe as they peacefully made their way into Istanbul. But the riot police had become more and more aggressive as the protests had carried on, using tear gas and water cannons to disperse the massive throngs of people in the streets.

On the third day of the protests, Ağa had found himself on the front lines, trying to help the injured away from the line of fire and into the nearest ambulances.

Trapped within the massive swell of people, crowded in on every side of his body, he had felt like a wildebeest caught in the thick of a giant stampede. But it wasn't the feeling of being crushed like a soda can that had filled Ağa with fear. It was the sounds he had heard as the riot police fired tear gas into the crowd — the sounds of people, ordinary people just like himself, crying, screaming, howling as they began to realize their attempts at resisting the iron-fisted regime were growing more and more futile by the second.

Lieutenant Ağa had witnessed plenty of bloodshed over the course of his thirty-year career. Seeing the occasional arm or leg that had been blown off by a pipe bomb was nothing that he ever lost sleep over. But it was the *sounds* — those awful, almost inhuman and bloodcurdling sounds — that kept him awake at night. And it was Zümra's face that kept flickering back into his memory, like a flame whisking gracefully around the wick of a candle, that made his heart squeeze so tight the feeling almost overpowered the pain in his arm.

She had been on the front lines, squaring off with a wall of heavily armed riot police, when she noticed Ağa in the crowd among her. He would never forget her brazen, steely eyes and her hawkish stare as he wriggled his way through the masses, looking to assess if anybody in need of medical attention required help fighting their way through the crowd to the EMTs.

He hadn't noticed her at first. He had finally secured a spot amongst the crowd when he noticed the young woman boring holes into him with her eyes. Her smile had been one of utter contempt.

"WHAT ARE YOU DOING here?" she asked, planting her feet firmly on the ground to withstand the jostling of the people around her. "Aren't you supposed to be on the other side with them?" She flicked her chin toward the line of riot police in front of them.

Ağa was immediately taken aback, not only by the brashness of her question but also at the woman's striking beauty. She stood tall and firm despite the chaos unraveling around her, like a tree amid a burning forest fire. Her nose was long and elegant, and her cheekbones rose high above her face like the slopes of the Taurus Mountains. Her hair was wrapped in an ornate turquoise scarf. He stared for a second too long before managing a response.

"I, uh — no," he grunted, scanning his surroundings in search of anyone on the ground. "I'm not here for riot control."

"Oh. So, you're here to arrest us individually, then?" she scoffed, her eyes piercing his body so sharply he thought he might go into cardiac arrest.

"I'm not here to arrest anybody," Ağa growled at her. Despite her radiance, she was getting under his skin. "I'm trying to make sure that nobody is hurt, and if they are, I'm getting them to an ambulance."

The woman's demeanor changed suddenly, her face softening as she gave the lieutenant a once-over with her burning, feverish gaze. She offered no apology but instead said, "Then I'm glad you're here. There was a young boy standing by me moments ago who looked badly hurt by the tear gas, but he disappeared. They're not going to stop until we're all blind. Or dead."

Her shoulder was suddenly smashed into by a riot officer's shield.

"Get back!" the officer yelled. The woman stumbled backwards. Ağa instinctively reached out to grab her before she hit the ground. He cradled the small of her back as he pulled her up by her forearm.

"*Hıyar!*" she spat at the officer who had slammed into her.

Ağa's eyes widened and quickly looked to make sure the riot officer hadn't heard the insult. It appeared that he didn't. He was busy hassling the next person who got too close to his shield. Ağa let go of the woman once she was steady on two feet again.

"Thank you," she said to Ağa, turning back to him with those fierce and fury-filled eyes. "You should go make sure no one else is hurt now."

She was right, but Ağa didn't want to go. He wanted to stay and be burned alive by the woman's stare.

"Are you hurt?" he asked. He felt like he was a shy and awkward high schooler again, grasping for words and trying to find any excuse to linger just a little bit longer and bask in the woman's presence.

"No," she responded coolly. "I'm fine. But there are people here who definitely are not."

Ağa shrugged in agreement and begun to meander off when another riot officer approached the woman. Before Ağa even had a chance to react, the officer's fist collided with full force into her cheekbone with a sickening crack. She fell onto her right arm and stayed motionless on the ground, her forehead to the pavement, her hair spilling out of the scarf that had come undone from her head with the force of the blow.

"We told you to stay back!" roared the officer, spittle spraying from the corners of his mouth. He looked like a rabid dog, teeth glinting in the afternoon sun.

Ağa's heart nearly jumped from his chest as he ran back towards her. Slowly, so as not to exacerbate any injuries, he turned her over to face him.

The woman's cheek was bruised and purple, but her forehead near her hairline was bleeding profusely. Thick red blood gushed from the wound and ran rivers down her face.

She looked unconscious, but Ağa could see her eyeballs fluttering underneath the lids. He breathed a sigh of relief.

"Hey," he muttered gently, "can you hear me?"

She groaned in response and then said, "I guess now I'm *really* glad that you're here."

Ağa chuckled softly. The crowd around him was getting more and more restless as the riot police continued with their brutal advances. He was being jostled from either side and was afraid if the woman stayed on the ground any longer, she would be trampled. "Can you stand up?"

She squeezed her eyes shut before opening them again, squinting into the glaring sun above her. "I think so," she managed.

Ağa pulled her from the ground and steadied her as they walked through the crowd to the side of the street. He asked the woman for her name.

"Zümra," she responded through gritted teeth, trying to avoid the flying fists and elbows of the protestors around them.

"And what do you do, Zümra?" Ağa pressed on, trying to keep her focused and talking. With a head injury like hers, he was afraid she might lose consciousness.

"I used to work in finance," she said, skirting to the right to avoid a glass bottle whizzing past her head. Ağa ducked as it shattered into pieces behind him. "But that's not important. Where is the nearest ambulance? The bleeding won't stop."

"Put your scarf on the wound and keep pressure on it," Ağa said. "We're almost there."

Zümra did as she was told and let Ağa lead her from the crowd to the edge of the street. There was not an ambulance in sight. Panic gripped Ağa's chest as he spun in circles looking for one. How could this be?

"I'm going to need to call for one," he finally said, pulling out his walkie-talkie, defeated. "Here. Sit down. And keep putting pressure on the wound." He motioned toward a bench on the sidewalk, where she sat, bent at the spine like a wilted flower begging for water.

"They'll be here soon," he said after making the call, clipping the radio back to his belt and kneeling down to inspect Zümra's wound. "Is there anyone you want me to call? Does your husband know you're here?"

"My husband," Zümra chortled, rolling her eyes, a subtle smile inching its way across her face from the corners of her mouth. "No. Thank you, Lieutenant. Nobody needs to know I've been here today."

Ağa nodded grimly in silence. He could still see the river of blood running down Zümra's face, a ribbon of crimson trickling through the canvas of golden skin. He and Zümra looked out wordlessly at the scene before them: riot officers throwing canisters of tear gas at an alarming rate, protestors returning fire with bottles and whatever else they could find on the street as a weapon. The sounds of people screaming in pain as they covered their eyes was almost too much for Ağa to bear.

"Is it too much to ask?" Zümra asked, furrowing her bloodstained brow and immediately flinching from the pain.

"What is?" Ağa responded, confused by the question.

"For civility. Human rights. Decency," she said, unblinking. "We just want a livable Turkey. Freedom of the press. The ability to organize. Democracy. And now look what it's all coming to. We shouldn't have to fight for this."

Ağa blew out a sigh in agreement. "I want a livable Turkey, too," he said. "That's why I joined the police force, at first. I thought it would be easy to change the system once I was in it. But it's been thirty years and still...look what it's all coming to," he echoed with a slight smile.

Zümra turned the scarf around on its other side. It was completely soaked through with blood. Ağa's forehead creased with worry.

"You're losing a lot of blood," he said warily. "Don't stop putting pressure on it."

"I'm not, I just —" Zümra faltered, swaying slightly. "I feel a little tired."

Alarm bells went off in Ağa's head.

"Stay awake, Zümra," he said, trying to keep his voice from sounding frantic. "You probably have a bad concussion. We need to wait for the ambulance to arrive before you can go to sleep. OK? Try and stay awake before then, please."

Zümra nodded, but Ağa noticed that she wasn't applying pressure to the wound anymore. He took the scarf from her and pressed onto her forehead for her. Her eyes fluttered closed.

"Stay awake," he said again, harshly this time. Her eyes snapped back open, and, for a brief and wonderfully blissful moment, Ağa felt like they had pierced directly through his body and into his soul. He looked away.

The ambulance arrived about five minutes later, but it had been a struggle to keep Zümra awake. She was leaning on his shoulder in half-consciousness by the time the EMTs picked her up and put her on a stretcher.

"Where are you taking her?" Ağa asked, feeling a surge of protectiveness over this brave and beautiful young woman. She had been standing so proud and tall in front of him just moments ago. Now, she looked like a deflated red balloon, drenched in her own blood, rapidly losing consciousness thanks to a riot officer with an inflated ego and giant knuckles to match. He really was a *hıyar*.

"*Özel Çapa Hastanesi* is closest," the young EMT responded. "Are you going to ride along?"

"I need to stay here," Ağa said with a grimace, looking back out into the sea of protestors clashing against the clear plastic shields of the riot police. He clenched his teeth and tried to focus on his breathing. "I'll call in the morning to make sure she's okay."

IN THE MORNING, THE doctor on the phone told Ağa the young woman had succumbed to her injuries. Subarachnoid hemorrhage. It was quick and painless and hard to detect. There was nothing more that they could have done for her.

Ağa didn't eat for two days after that. He couldn't get her words out of his head. They followed him wherever he went: to the bakery in the mornings, where he bought his *simit* and coffee, in the blare of the police car's sirens as he sped down the street, in the monotonous drone of the news on the TV in the station's lobby.

"We shouldn't have to fight for this."

And yet, she had — and she had lost her life because of it.

It had truly been a summer of incessant unrest. The violence was already outrageous enough *without* a killer robot aiding the military police. Ağa didn't want to imagine what would happen should a weapon of this caliber be unleashed on huge groups of civilians. The rage and the pain of losing Zümra, along with countless other innocent civilians that he had sworn to protect, was still searing unbearably in his chest.

Ceylan had followed him inside his office. He looked deeply troubled.

"Lieutenant," he said. "Two things. One, you're bleeding."

Ağa looked down at his arm and watched indifferently as a pool of crimson blood blossomed across the fresh white bandage.

"Two," Ceylan continued. "We just got a call from the Cengelkoy Sabanci Police Center, over in Üsküdar. They were notified early this morning of a couple of kids who broke into *Beylerbeyi Sarayı*. Look." He stepped forward and slapped a photograph onto Ağa's desk. "This is a snapshot from the palace's security cameras. Do you recognize anyone?"

Ağa squinted. The image was blurry. Whoever was going through the frame was moving at remarkable speed. Yet as his eyes focused, he realized he was looking at the tail end of a blur of black hair in the wind.

"Azar," he murmured, the rage in his body suddenly turning to rising elation.

"That's what I thought," Ceylan responded. "It looks like she's being swept away by something. But at least we have a lead. We know she's on the other side of the Bosphorus."

"When was this picture taken?" Ağa frantically searched around his workspace for something he could wrap around his arm to slow the bleeding. The bandage was soaked almost entirely through.

"Six-oh-two this morning," Ceylan said, raising an eyebrow with growing concern at Ağa's battered state. He pulled off his jacket and held it out to the lieutenant. Ağa snatched it out of his hand and started hysterically twisting it around his tricep.

"Shit," he said, pulling on one of the jacket sleeves to tighten its grip on his arm. "That was eight hours ago. They could be halfway on their way to Sultanbeyli by now."

Ceylan took the photograph from the desk again and slipped it into his back pocket. "Do you, uh...do you want me to get help?"

Ağa shook his head, agitated. "Does the *Askeri İnzibat* know about this?"

"What? That you're bleeding profusely from your arm and should probably go to the hospital to get it checked out?"

"No," Ağa snapped, flaring his nostrils at the young officer before him. "Ceylan, we don't have time to mess around. There's something seriously dangerous on the loose, and it happens to have taken a pause from its killing spree to kidnap Azar Şamdereli. Does the *Askeri İnzibat* know that Azar was spotted at *Beylerbeyi Sarayı* this morning?"

Ceylan blinked. "No, sir," he replied. "As far as I know, we're the only police station in Istanbul that's been employed on this mission to help. They're keeping this largely undercover and haven't let the other stations know of their presence here."

"Good. From now on, any more information we acquire about Azar or the robot stays between us," Ağa said, leaning on his desk with his good arm and staring down at the mess of papers in front of him. He paused before standing upright again to meet Ceylan's eyes. "I need you to get Topuz and Officer Parlak, now. Meet back in my office as quickly as possible."

Ceylan's eyes widened, but he didn't say anything. He nodded and turned to leave the room.

"Oh. And Ceylan?" Ağa grimaced, leaning back on the desk with his good arm. "Can you see if Hiranur still has some of that Vicodin left over from her oral surgery? I'm going to pass out if I don't get some painkillers soon."

Ceylan shot the lieutenant a small smile and disappeared behind the door.

Chapter Twenty

June 19, 2017

Professor Çakır Müjde yawned and reached for the cup of tea on her desk.

It was past 1:30 in the morning, and her eyes, sleepy and drooping behind the thick lenses of her big round glasses, were starting to glaze over. The blue light radiating from her computer felt hot and irritating on her skin. She feared the long days and nights staring at her screen were beginning to show on her face.

The cup was empty. Irritated, she stood up to leave and sighed. Perhaps this was a sign that she should go home. She slung her messenger bag over her shoulder and clicked off the lights. She had an eight-a.m. lecture scheduled for tomorrow morning. Closing the door behind her, she briefly debated texting her graduate assistant and asking him to give the lesson so she could sleep in.

Professor Müjde lived just a short walk from the university. In what seemed like a strike of good fortune, she had secured a new apartment in the surrounding Serencebey neighborhood just days after accepting the offer to teach the undergraduate molecular genetics seminar. She and her fiancé, Stefan, had been living in Berlin, both working as lecturers at Humboldt University, when Yıldız had reached out. The pay was decent, and the weather in Istanbul was much better than it was in northern Germany, so they had taken the leap to move to Turkey together. It felt good to be back in her home country. The daily calls to prayer, the smell of spices wafting from the bazaars through the air — everything was familiar and warm, a stark contrast to Berlin's cold and gray.

Rounding the corner from F Blok, Müjde cut through the mechanical engineering department to the nearest exit to the street. The air was still warm on her skin. She flicked on her iPhone flashlight, silently cursing the university for never having installed more lamps on the pathway from F Blok over to E Blok and the street.

A slight rustling in the bushes by the mechanical engineering building jolted her gaze up from her phone. Likely, it was a stray cat rummaging the grounds for a juicy mouse. There were plenty of strays in this area at night.

But that wasn't what caught Müjde's attention. She frowned, shining her light at the building and walking over for a closer look.

Someone had left the hall light on.

Could it be the janitor? she wondered, making her way around the building to the back door to see if it was open.

She could see just a sliver of light coming through the crack of the door left slightly ajar. The crease in her brow deepened. She knew that there was a janitor who worked night shifts, but he didn't usually start until later in the morning, around four. Cautiously, she opened the door and peered down the narrow staircase leading to the basement.

Müjde strained to listen for if there was anything going on inside the lab. She had said goodbye to all the professors of the research group earlier that evening. As far as she knew, there wasn't anyone else that was supposed to be working late tonight.

Not a sound came up from the basement. İnan had probably fallen asleep down there during one of his later shifts. She quietly descended the stairs and turned left.

The door to the laboratory was locked. Puzzled, Müjde took a step back. Why would the door to the building be open, but the room locked? Was there someone working in another lab inside the building this late?

Müjde hated the thought of İnan spending another night in the basement all alone, slumped in a cold, plastic chair too small for his large, stocky build. He was a good kid. Since he'd joined the team, she'd felt riddled with guilt at his involvement in such a precarious and dangerous experiment. She took out her key and quietly unlocked the door.

The computers were humming low and steady in their sleep, and the light was on, but İnan was nowhere in sight. Müjde checked underneath the tables, one eyebrow creeping up her forehead. Perhaps he had just forgotten to turn off the hallway light and close the door on his way out tonight.

She was ready to turn around and head back up the stairs when she realized the door to the room in the far corner was open just a crack. A sinking feeling settled in her stomach. No one had been authorized to do any work on the robot tonight. If there was somebody in the room, it couldn't have been someone from the research team. Had they been discovered by an outsider?

Tiptoeing across the laboratory, Müjde gathered all the courage she could muster and peeked through the tiny gap into the room.

There was nothing she could do to keep her jaw from falling as she threw the door open in astonishment. Words failed her as she stared, wild-eyed like a spooked horse, into the room.

"Mustafa," she finally stammered, her heart racing through her chest. "What in God's name are you doing down here?"

Chapter Twenty-One

August 20, 2017

Azar had never been on the run from the authorities before, much less accompanied by an autonomous killer robot, to find shelter among the final resting place of absolute strangers in Karacaahmet Cemetery. But there was a first time for everything.

Fleeing from place to place without a set plan or clear direction in which she was headed was grinding on Azar. Suddenly having to play by ear was terribly nerve-wracking, and she grew more and more restless as the hours dragged on. It still felt like every time she picked up a piece of critical information, another piece slipped through her fingers, like a fish writhing to escape from the grasp of a fisherman.

The cemetery was sprawling, and there were plenty of places to hide should somebody follow them here. She tried not to let the tombstones towering above her unsettle her as she and Manti nestled underneath a large pine on the outskirts of the grounds.

Mustafa had wished to be cremated upon his death. He had requested his ashes to be scattered from the hills in Hayriye, where he was born. Azar wondered if Ediz had received the ashes from the crematorium yet. She scanned the cemetery, her eyes warily landing on each tombstone, reading the names, the dates, the prayers inscribed into the cold, gray stone. She shuddered.

What a strange concept it was—to be alive and then suddenly not to be. You were awake and breathing one moment, and the next, you weren't, and you wouldn't even realize what had happened. You'd be gone and at peace, without a care in the world for what happened next because you were dead. But suddenly, there would be a massive hole ripped in the lives of those left behind — an awful, unpatchable, gut-wrenching hole that, no matter how hard they'd try to zip it closed for fear of never feeling quite whole again, would find a way to burst back open and spill out its awful contents of fear and loneliness and devastation.

Azar hadn't realized that tears had started to spill down her face until she heard Manti's tinny, mechanic voice say, "You are hurt."

She quickly wiped away the tears with her sleeve and chuckled. A steady breeze had started to make the low-hanging branches of the pine tree fan gently at her long black hair. "Yes," she said, turning to face the robot. "How do you know that?"

Manti's eyes on the left side of its face whirled, but the rest stood still.

"I compute tears. And tears are a sign of anguish," Manti said. "But you do not have a wound. Where does it hurt?"

Azar managed a slight chuckle. "No, I don't have a wound. I'm okay. Sometimes, humans need to cry when they are hurt. emotionally hurt. Our memories, our feelings – they can cause us pain. It's not something that comes from a wound, but it hurts all the same."

The rest of Manti's eyes resumed their whirling. "You are able to feel anguish, even when you are not wounded," it said.

Azar felt that Manti was beginning to open up, little by little. It was almost as if it were evolving — learning from its previous experiences to form new ones and making its decisions based on that information. Like a human.

How absolutely fascinating.

"You're good at learning from your environment," Azar replied, tearing a piece of grass from the ground and ripping the thin blade apart with her hands. Her stomach growled. She realized she'd been too overloaded on adrenaline to feel hunger before, but it had been over fifteen hours since she'd last eaten.

"Yes," Manti responded cheerfully. Azar wished that someone had thought to program the robot's voice so its tone would fluctuate, rather than sounding so high-pitched and happy all the time.

A slow, sad smile crept its away across Azar's face. Trying to keep more tears from welling up in her eyes, she asked, "Do you remember anything about how it all began? Can you tell me about it?"

The robot didn't respond right away.

"Is there anything at all that you know about how you were created? And why?" she tried again. "You must remember something, no?"

"I am programmed to hunt," came the response from the machine.

"So I've noticed." Azar felt a twinge of fear slice through her gut.

"I was tethered to the lifegiver," the robot continued, "and it fed me what I needed to survive. I am full of its lifefluid."

"You — you what?" Azar hadn't expected this answer in the slightest. Full of lifefluid?

"I am full of its lifefluid," Manti repeated. "I know not to allow any punctures to my outer casing. Otherwise, it might spill out of my circulatory system."

"Your circulatory system," Azar repeated, nearly dumbstruck. "So, you have a heart? And veins? This fluid is essentially your blood?"

Her mind suddenly flashed back to the picture Ağa had shown her what seemed like decades ago. Amid the wreckage of the laboratory, there had been a mysterious dried liquid on the floor. Was that the lifefluid the robot was referring to?

Suddenly, the pieces fit together perfectly in her head. "You were engineered with the DNA of animals," she said. "You have blood — and it's full of that DNA and flows through your circulatory system. That's why you have such sharp hunting instincts." Azar beamed inwardly at this small yet monumental milestone. She was one step closer to finding out what she was really dealing with.

"That is correct," Manti said. Its eyes spun and spun their never-ending circles.

"And the lifegiver...it was a chamber that pumped you full of the fluid," Azar continued, eyeing the robot to gauge whether she was still heading in the right direction with this. "Did it pump it through that hole in your stomach?"

"Yes."

"How did you get loose? And why?" she asked, fearing the answer would be something she wasn't ready to hear.

"I felt hunger," the robot responded, somehow cheery as always. "I was ready to hunt."

Azar tried not to let any emotion show on her face as she processed this information.

It made sense. It was only a matter of time before something programmed to hunt and kill would break from its bindings and follow its given instincts. The robot had behaved just like any other predator would.

"I'm curious," she said slowly, "what exactly you're made up of. I can tell you've got some sort of large cat in you. Maybe a lion, or a tiger. But what else?"

The movement of Manti's clicking eyes became more abrupt. They looked like the gears of a machine whose rotation was thwarted by something stuck in between them.

"I do not know," Manti said.

Azar tried not to let disappointment overwhelm her. She sat back against the trunk of the pine tree and sighed, flinging the blade of grass and watching it blow in the wind across the lawn.

"Why have you not hunted me?" she asked meagerly, turning back to face the robot next to her.

Manti stared straight ahead.

"I do not know," it said again.

The blade of grass fell gracefully out from the talons of the wind, disappearing among the grayscale quilt of the cemetery's scattered tombstones.

Chapter Twenty-Two

August 20, 2017

There was already a throng of tourists outside the palace's main gate by the time Lieutenant Ağa reached *Beylerbeyi Sarayı*. They shuffled awkwardly amongst each other, hoisting high their selfie sticks and snapping pictures as they waited for clearance to be let in.

"Excuse me," he mumbled, pushing through the crowd toward the building, leading with his right shoulder. He was flanked by Officers Ceylan, Topuz, and Parlak, a broad-shouldered woman with a round, red face and the straightest, whitest teeth Ağa had ever seen in his life. Parlak was a veteran in the department and was often assigned on cases involving kidnappings and missing persons.

"Excuse me, police," he mumbled again at a large family of Americans standing obliviously in his path. The two teenage girls were taking selfies in front of the palace's staircase to the main entrance. Neither of them acknowledged him until they finished snapping the photo. They dispersed in a fit of giggles once they noticed the group of officers in front of them.

Ağa rolled his eyes and climbed up the steps to the main doorway. He had created a sling from Ceylan's jacket for his arm and knew he probably looked ridiculous, though none of his team members had said anything to him. He had other things to worry about at the moment.

A security officer was standing at the top, scanning the surroundings.

"Lieutenant Ağa, Beşiktaş," he grunted at the guard, flashing his badge and reaching for his tobacco to roll a cigarette. It was an exceedingly difficult task to complete with one hand. "We got a call about a break-in early this morning."

The security guard was an older gentleman, possibly in his late sixties, who stood with a small hunch in his back like a shepherd's cane. When he took off his sunglasses, Ağa noticed one of his eyes was blind, scarred, blue and nearly translucent.

"Hello, Lieutenant Ağa," the security guard said. "Yes, that's right. Thank you for coming down. I'll have someone bring you in. We were just conducting a final sweep to allow tourists back into the building. It seems the intruders didn't take anything last night. They just broke in the back door and left."

The security guard took out a walkie-talkie and started calling for someone to meet the officers at the front gate.

"Odd. Can you show us the security footage?" Ağa asked, sucking in a drag of cigarette smoke.

The security guard nodded. "Someone is coming now to get you."

A tall man with slicked-back hair and fierce black eyebrows met them at the front steps. He wore a pink button-up shirt and a name tag that read BARIŞ BOZGÜNEY, GROUNDSKEEPER.

"This way, please," he said and ushered the police officers into the palace.

Ağa marveled at the high, ornate ceilings glittering with beautiful Bohemian chandeliers. The floors were covered in a thick, luxurious red carpet. Not a single centimeter of the walls was left untouched by the handsome paintings of vines and blossoms intertwining across the halls. Elegant Iznik vases stood proudly on the mahogany tables. Topuz let out a soft whistle.

Bozgüney opened a door in the far corner of the main parlor and led the police officers into the security room. Dozens of TV monitors lined the walls.

"We're not sure how they were able to open the door," the man said, leaning over one of the machines and frantically clicking on the mouse again and again, "and what's even more confusing is that they were able to disable the alarm before it could notify us someone was in the building. It's supposed to send us a signal right away." The man shrugged. "Perhaps there was a bug in the system."

"I don't think it was your alarm," Ağa murmured, leaning in to one of the TV monitors and squinting at the screen.

Bozgüney let out a chuckle. "Well, if it wasn't the alarm, then something definitely went wrong with the security cameras. This is all we captured from last night. Whoever was in here was moving so fast that we couldn't see them go by. Even if we slow the footage down, it's too dark to clearly make out a face."

Ağa didn't say anything. Everyone stared wordlessly at the screens as they watched white streaks flash across them.

Behind him, Topuz slowly pulled a banana out of his jacket pocket and began to peel it.

Ceylan was the first one to speak. "And they left the building at six this morning?" he asked, pulling out a notepad and pen. Ağa's eyes were still glued to the monitors. Why would the robot bring Azar into a historical palace and then leave again suddenly? None of its behavior was making sense.

"Yes. It appears they decided to stay the night," Bozgüney said. He crossed his arms, immediately putting wrinkles into his pink button-up, and shook his head. "I'm honestly impressed at how someone could pull something like this off. My best guess is that it was some kind of school prank, no more than a bunch of teenagers messing around. But your guess is as good as mine as to how they got past the security precautions."

"Did anybody see them leave the building?" Ağa asked, finally tearing his gaze from the screens and looking at the man again. "Any idea as to which direction they were headed?"

"I asked our security guard who came in early this morning," Bozgüney replied, uncrossing his arms again. "He said he saw some movement along the water, heading toward Fıstıkağacı, but he couldn't exactly pinpoint who or what it was." The groundskeeper's demeanor suddenly changed as he glanced at the group of officers, one bushy eyebrow raised like a caterpillar on his forehead. "He did tell the officers who were here this morning about that already, though. I'm assuming you are here to collect fingerprints and search the building one more time?"

At this, Ağa whipped his head back to Ceylan, Topuz, and Parlak standing behind him. Topuz stopped peeling the banana. "What?" he hissed, eyes darting from one officer to the next for any sign of reassurance that what he feared was incorrect. All of them met his eyes with blank, unintelligible stares. "Was somebody from Beşiktaş or Cengelkoy Sabanci here earlier today?"

"Oh, no. They weren't municipal police officers," Bozgüney said slowly, unsure of how to react to this suddenly uncomfortable situation he found himself in. "They were *Askeri İnzibat*. Surely they were the ones who assigned you to take a look at the case?"

Despite the Vicodin pills he had taken earlier, Ağa's left arm began throbbing with vicious pain.

"We need to go," he said, gritting his teeth and starting for the door. "They're already kilometers ahead of us. If they catch this thing before we do, our entire country is screwed."

AZAR WAS TREMBLING. It was getting close to 3, and she was hungry, sleep-deprived, and constantly on edge for fear of being ripped to shreds by the killer robot she had accidentally somewhat befriended. She leaned against the trunk of the pine tree and felt the tears streaming down her cheeks again.

"I can sense your fear," the robot quipped out of nowhere. Azar did a double take. This thing had killer instincts, both for hunting and for reading a room.

"I'm — I'm not afraid," she retorted. She tore another blade of grass from the soil and suddenly laughed. What was the point of trying to lie?

"Well, yes. Yes, I am," she snorted, ripping the blade of grass in half and throwing the two pieces back to the ground. "I'm afraid that the police are going to find us and destroy you before I discover your true purpose. I'm afraid that you might turn on me and kill me like you did my father. And

I'm afraid because I have absolutely no idea what I'm doing or what I'm dealing with and how this is all going to end. It's like I'm swimming in the ocean at night, with no lights anywhere — just swimming, wondering when the next time I'm going to find land is. I'm aimlessly floating, trying to keep my head above water with no sense of a plan, and it's terrifying."

The words spilled out of her like rocks tumbling down a mountainside during an avalanche.

"And not only that, I'm swimming with a shark." She laughed again. "I'm not good at doing things without some sort of direction."

Manti's eyes came to a halt.

"Your father?" it asked slowly.

Azar nodded. The tears were rushing down her face in rivers now. "Yeah," she said, sniffing loudly. "He helped create you. He helped create *me.* He was *my* lifegiver."

There was such a burning tension in the air — *could the robot even feel tension, if it was able to feel fear and pain in other people?* — that Azar put her head between her knees, unable to look at the robot next to her.

Manti's eyes started twirling again, as if it were slowly computing something in its artificially intelligent mind. Azar heard a clicking sound — the same one the robot emitted when it learned a new word.

"You feel pain and fear," the robot said. "And you have lost your father."

Azar nodded wordlessly, her head still tucked between her knees. When she looked back up, Manti was staring out into the distance, its eyes slowly drawing their melancholy circles on its expressionless face.

Chapter Twenty-Three

August 20, 2017

Underneath the pine tree at the Karacaahmet Cemetery, a prickling sensation slowly snaked its way through Manti's core.

The robot was sitting next to Azar, processing her each and every word, slowly beginning to develop an understanding of her deeply complex and intelligent mind. She kept asking it questions it did not know the answer to. It wished it could be of more use to her. But whenever Azar asked something about what it was feeling, there was a blank within its processing system, like someone had wiped its memory disc completely clean.

The prickling sensation began to grow stronger. Manti shifted, eyes clicking as it brought its focus from its peripherals and back to Azar. She was looking out into the distance, black hair waving softly in the gentle breeze. The young woman looked troubled, as if she were pondering the answer to an important and life-altering question. Streams of fresh tears glistened on her cheekbones.

There was a certain warmth inside its core that Manti had sensed before. It was strange and distant, yet wonderful at the same time. It was that same pulse of electricity it had felt underneath the bridge, before it had gone back to the university to find Azar, when it realized she was in danger.

There was more to this odd sensation than just warmth. Instantly, Manti realized what it was feeling was something it was very, very familiar with.

It was hunger.

Slowly, the robot's claws began unsheathing themselves from their cases.

Chapter Twenty-Four

August 20, 2017

O fficer Demirci looked at her watch and frowned.
It was already 3:45. How had the day passed her by so quickly already?

Thanks to the phone call the *Askeri İnzibat* had intercepted between the Cengelkoy Sabanci and Beşiktaş police stations, she'd been tipped off as to the robot's location early this morning. She was glad Lieutenant Ağa had still been unconscious in his hospital bed when the call was made. It had given her and her team a few extra hours to get to the palace and search the area.

However, by the time they had arrived, there was no sign of the robot anywhere near *Beylerbeyi Sarayı*. The security guard had mentioned seeing something running in the direction of the Fıstıkağacı metro station, so she and the team had split up around the neighborhood in search of any signs of the robot's appearance. So far, they were out of luck. Demirci felt like she had scoured the entire shoreline of Üsküdar twice over, and not once had her tracker blinked.

Jamaković and two other *Askeri İnzibat* officers had gone further southwest, toward Doğancılar and Harem. Still three more had ventured east. Nobody had picked up a single clue as to where the robot may have gone. Tired of feeling like a dog chasing its own tail, Demirci decided to make a pit stop at the nearest cafe.

Demirci had never liked the way the mood would shift as soon as she stepped into a public place, wearing her unmistakable helmet and uniform. Restaurants, cafes, public transportation — when she was in uniform, these all became places that instantly felt cold and uninviting. She could understand why having a military police officer with a giant machine gun strapped to her body would make some people feel uncomfortable, but she was just here to do her job — to serve her government and collect her paycheck. Today, she needed a strong kick of caffeine in order to do her job well.

A hush fell over the cafe as she opened the door. She was suddenly aware of how loud her combat boots clomped on the ground when she walked. With a brisk nod, she stepped up to the counter and ordered a *sade kahve*. Despite the bitterness of Turkish coffee, she never took it with sweetener.

Demirci sat at a table by the far window and tried to think, not letting the uncomfortable gazes from fellow patrons bother her. Where could the robot be hiding in broad daylight? And why had it, seemingly randomly, stopped wreaking bloodshed on innocent civilians?

A pair of men in their late sixties or early seventies were sitting at the table across from Demirci, bowed over a chessboard, deep in thought. The man wearing the half-moon glasses and a cotton cap plucked his opponent's bishop from the board with a swoop of his queen. The opponent, a portly, balding man wearing a colorful vest, cried out in surprise.

"That's what happens when you don't pay attention," said the man wearing glasses, laughing. He placed the bishop next to his other spoils of war on the side of the table.

"*Allah askina*, I was!" the portly man grumbled, trying to hide the smile tugging at the corner of his mouth.

"Your mind is somewhere else," his friend said, grinning.

The server came out from behind the counter and placed the steaming black coffee in front of Demirci. She cupped it between her hands and looked down at her own reflection staring at her from the rich, dark liquid.

The stout man sighed. "Yes, you're right. I'm thinking about Yusuf. I saw him this morning and I'm a little concerned. Do you know what he said to me?"

"What?" the other man said without letting his eyes leave the chessboard.

"He said he went to visit Eylül at the cemetery today," he replied, picking up a knight and shuffling it across the black and white squares.

"So? It's normal for people to visit the graves of their spouses," said the man in the half-moon glasses and the cotton cap. "Why be concerned?" He obliterated the knight with one fell swoop of his rook.

"*Allah askina!*" the stout man in the vest cried again. He looked up at his opponent sitting across the table. "Listen to me, Muhammed. Yusuf has always been a very spiritual man, but I'm concerned for him because he said he saw her ghost today."

Muhammed finally looked up from the board in surprise, his half-moon glasses sliding further down the bridge of his long, hooked nose. "He what?"

The other man nodded and lowered his voice to a whisper. Demirci shifted in her seat, closer to the two men, and attempted to subtly listen in.

"He said he saw her briefly, just as he was leaving the cemetery. He saw a flash of white and long, black hair pass by him. He even felt the breeze as she went by. He was sure it was her spirit that had come to see him."

Demirci froze, bent halfway out of her seat toward her shoe that didn't actually need tying. A flash of white with long black hair? That sounded vaguely familiar.

"Excuse me, gentlemen," she said, rising from her seat and pushing the machine gun onto her back so as not to startle them too greatly. They both looked at her in surprise, as if they'd never realized she had sat down in the first place.

"I'm sorry to interrupt your game, but I overheard a snippet of your conversation. Which cemetery was it where your friend saw the ghost?"

The men stared blankly at her in stunned silence. Demirci flashed them a toothy grin and said, "I am a public safety officer, as you can see. I can't be letting ghosts running loose around the city."

The bald man stuttered a reply. "Yes, of course. I believe he was at Karacaahmet. Right, Muhammed? That's where Eylül is buried?" He turned back to look at the man in glasses, who nodded.

"Yes, I think that's right."

"Thank you, gentlemen," Demirci said, reaching for her walkie-talkie and starting out the door. "Again, I'm sorry to disturb."

The men didn't respond but watched in confused silence as the officer disappeared out of the cafe.

"Your move," Muhammed finally said, turning his attention back to the board.

Demirci whipped out her phone and Googled directions to Karacaahmet Cemetery. It was only a few kilometers away. She decided to walk rather than retrieve her car from the waterfront and drive over. The traffic was starting to become miserable anyhow.

"Rahmi, do you copy?" she barked into the walkie-talkie. There was a brief moment of static before the officer responded.

"Yes, I'm here. Any news?" came Jamaković's staticky voice over the radio.

"I have a lead. Meet me at the Karacaahmet Cemetery as quickly as possible. There's a very slight chance somebody saw the robot with Azar there earlier today."

"Roger that," said Jamaković. "I'll be there with Mataraci and Uzun in fifteen minutes."

Demirci hustled to the cemetery, weaving through the streets teeming with people visiting the fish markets and spice shops on their way home from work. She kept her eyes on the tracker as she made her way over, watching for any sign of the red dot to appear on the screen.

Jamaković and the other officers were already waiting at the front gate by the time she arrived. The officers saluted each other before Demirci spoke.

"This is our best guess as to where they were this morning," she said, putting her hand back down to her side. "Have any of you detected it on your trackers?"

Mataraci, one of their younger officers with a clean-shaven face and a slightly cleft chin, nodded wordlessly. He held out his tracker to Demirci. She snatched it from his hand and frowned, silently cursing the fact that the trackers were still severely underdeveloped. Her device hadn't detected anything.

Sure enough, there was a red dot blinking on the corner of the map, all the way across the grounds towards the west. It seemed as if the robot was staying absolutely still.

Perfect.

"We need to go in quickly and *silently*," Demirci said in a hushed whisper, handing the tracker back to Mataraci. "The robot has excellent visual and auditory processing systems. One misstep and it will sense that we're here. Follow my every order and keep your wits about you. *Do not* shoot at it unless you absolutely have to."

The three men nodded and swiftly followed Demirci through the cemetery gate.

Chapter Twenty-Five

August 20, 2017

Manti perked up out of nowhere, shifting from all fours back onto two legs. Its eyes spun incessantly, faster now than they had before.

"What's going on?" Azar said, rising from the ground to stand next to it. She felt dizzy getting up. She needed food — or water at the very least. She tried to keep herself from imagining eating a fresh, warm *dürüm* as she scanned the cemetery grounds.

"I can sense movement," the robot replied. "There is a group of people approaching."

Azar tried to stay in control of her fear, but she felt it slowly begin to overpower her.

"Can you tell who they are?" she asked. Azar hoped with all her might that Lieutenant Ağa was among them. She still had no idea if the lieutenant had survived the attack. Had her phone not died hours ago, she would have called the station to make sure.

"No," Manti said, "but I can sense danger. They are coming towards us quickly. We need to move."

Azar nodded. If the police were after them with their tracking devices and machine guns, the best option was to take off running — in any direction — and worry about where to hide later. She needed to put as much distance as possible between them.

"Manti," she started but stopped abruptly. She hadn't noticed this before, but the robot's claws were out, their razor-sharp steel glinting in the afternoon sun. The robot was on the defense.

"We need to go," she said slowly, whipping her head back and forth in search of the best possible exit route. "We don't need to stay and fight. Let's move."

The robot was silent, save for the sound of its eyes whirring. The rest of its body stood absolutely motionless. Azar could sense it was processing something, but she was terrified of finding out what that could be.

"Let's go," she tried again. "Manti, they are going to hurt you. We need to leave."

"No," Manti chirped. "It's too late."

Azar's heart beat savagely against her ribcage like a bird trapped within a house made of glass. A cold sweat broke out on the back of her neck. Something wasn't right. There was no way it was too late for them to make a break for it. Considering the robot's incredible speed, they would have had plenty of time to escape without being seen.

It was stalling on purpose.

Azar stared at Manti's long, impossibly sharp claws and shuddered. She was rooted to the spot, unsure about her next move.

So, the robot was capable of deception. Would it try and stop her if she ran away and let the robot fend for itself?

Azar was suddenly startled by a rustling from the bushes across the pathway. She turned to the left and stared in horror as four police officers, all donning the signature *Askeri İnzibat* camouflage uniforms and helmets, emerged onto the path. Each of them carried a machine gun that seemed was twice the size of Azar's body.

She and Manti stepped out from underneath the pine tree and into the open air. Azar recognized the shorter officer in the front of the group, as well as the giant one behind the woman. The other two men were unfamiliar. Her heart sank when she realized that Ağa was not with them.

"Azar, are you okay?" Officer Demirci called out to her as the group approached steadily, weapons drawn and at the ready.

"Yes," she said meekly, unsure of whether Demirci was able to hear her. Manti had still not moved an inch.

"Are you hurt anywhere?" Demirci asked. The officers paused a few meters in front of Manti and Azar, not once letting their weapons drop.

"No," she said, trying to keep her voice from shaking. "I'm fine. I — please, don't shoot at it. I'm making good progress with it."

Demirci gave her an inquisitive look. "Progress?" she asked. "What does that mean?"

"I've been learning more about it and...and the way that it was programmed. It's capable of learning, and I don't want to see it destroyed," Azar replied. Cautiously, she took a step forward towards the officers.

Demirci snorted. "That's not up to you to decide," she said, "but we're not going to destroy it unless we have to. Step away from it, please."

Azar closed her eyes, seeking momentary tranquility within the space between her eyebrows. She couldn't let them take the robot away now. She had been making so much headway.

"I can't," she said, opening her eyes again at the officers. "I need to know everything before you take it away."

The beauty mark under Demirci's lip jumped as the officer's face twisted into a strange hybrid between a sneer and a frown.

"Azar *hanım,* don't make this more difficult than it already is," Demirci said icily. "This is not a game. Step away from it."

Azar knew that Manti could sense her agitation and tried to stifle it. The last thing she needed now was to escalate the situation.

Manti moved in half the time that Azar took to blink an eye.

With a massive whirring sound, it lunged at the group of officers. Demirci yelled something incoherent, and a shot rang out. Azar screamed and ducked onto the ground for cover.

Another *pang pang pang* reverberated as the machine guns ripped forth their unrelenting bullets. She heard what sounded like metal trash lids being slammed against each other like a pair of cymbals.

Azar peeked up from the ground. Almost immediately, she wished she hadn't.

Manti looked relatively unscathed. Other than a few scratches on its right side, it seemed to have gone untouched by the bullets, and the rain of gunfire only seemed to embolden it. But with one horrendous swing of its arm, Manti slashed its claws clean through the tall, skinny officer's midsection. The man cried out in agony and fell backwards, blood fountaining from his belly and into a pool on the dirt path.

Horrified, Azar squeezed her eyes shut again and curled as tightly as she could into a ball on the ground. There was no way a person could have survived getting sliced almost in half like that. She choked back tears. The other officers were shouting, but she couldn't understand what they were saying. More bullets ripped from the guns as she heard their voices grow distant, but Manti remained unperturbed. Azar heard another yell from the officer on the ground, followed by a horrible ripping sound.

Suddenly, everything went quiet.

When she opened her eyes again and looked up, Manti was standing above the fallen officer, its spinning eyes grinding to a halt. The man wasn't moving anymore.

The tears fell freely now. Azar's blurry vision was stained red from the blood that had spilled all over the pathway. Nausea gripped at her stomach, but she tried to swallow it down.

Calmly, Manti walked back to where she was curled up into a ball. Her forehead was pressed to the grass so hard she could feel the blades making imprints in her skin. Blood dripped from the robot's claws onto the lawn next to her. It cocked its head with that awful, unnatural, puppet-like movement.

"You are hurt," Manti remarked.

Slowly, it made its way back underneath the pine tree.

Chapter Twenty-Six

August 20, 2017

Azar's mind raced as she remained curled on the grass, unable to move, her breath coming in short, frantic gasps as she tried to get a hold of herself. She couldn't believe what had just unfolded in front of her eyes. The nausea still rippled through her body, pulsing and dancing in waves like a terrible electric current.

She felt incredibly stupid.

How could she have thought, even for an instant, that the robot was beginning to make progress and evolve into a somewhat civilized and intelligent being? No matter how docile or domesticated a natural predator may be, it was *always* to be treated like a dangerous animal. Those who didn't follow that rule and tried befriending lions or killer whales or whatever the thing might be usually ended up getting killed by it.

But she really *had* recognized signs of growth within the robot's behavior. Maybe it had just been a lapse of judgment. It was unreasonable to assume the robot could ignore every instinctive urge it had been programmed with.

She sobbed. Everything was falling apart. She had just witnessed a bloodbath that, though it pained her to think of this, was likely similar to the way her father had perished. The officers would come back for her, and this time, they'd be ready to capture and destroy the robot with every last bullet in those awful machine guns. There was absolutely no way she could get such a powerful force under control.

If she ran now, would Manti continue its killing spree on innocent victims? She pondered the way it had approached her, blood dripping from its claws and staining its white metal shell, as she lay on the grass just moments ago.

"You are hurt," it said again before disappearing back underneath the skirt of the pine tree.

Not only did Manti seem completely uninterested in killing her, but it also was incredibly in tune with what she was feeling.

It made no sense. Yet somehow, Azar recognized this as a sign that if there really was any hope for getting this thing under wraps, it was her.

She stood up, lowering her eyes to avoid the gruesome, gutted body splayed out on the path in front of her. Knees wobbling, she tucked herself back underneath the pine tree and gave Manti a good, long stare-down.

A memory flashed before her eyes and then left again as quickly as it had come.

At the end of high school, Azar's father had helped her with her university entrance exams, holding up flash cards and giving her words of encouragement in those critical moments when it felt like her brain was failing her and the world was falling apart.

"I don't even know if this is worth it," she had wailed, putting her head down on the kitchen table on her textbook.

"What if nothing that I'm working for turns out? I don't know if I can ever be a good teacher."

Mustafa had smiled and set the flash cards down next to her.

"Azar," he had said, "you're not always going to have a sense of the way things pan out. You just have to ride the wave and trust that it's taking you in the right direction."

She had been confused by this at the time, but suddenly, staring down at the impossible machine in front of her, it started to make sense.

There was no use in trying to wrestle with a wave that had pulled her under. She had to ride it and wait until she could put her head above water to breathe again. She had to trust the process, no matter how daunting it may be.

"Let's go," she said firmly, wiping the tears from her face with her sleeve.

The manticore's eyes clicked with a flash of fervor.

Chapter Twenty-Seven

August 20, 2017

Outside of the gate to the east entrance of the cemetery, Officer Demirci crouched to one knee and gasped, her entire body shaking with rage and desolation. Mataraci and Uzun flanked her on either side, standing over her wordlessly as she balled her shaking hand into a fist and bit down hard onto her knuckles.

"Call for backup," she spat quietly, seething. "We need to get Rahmi's body out of there and block the place off. And we need to find this thing before it gets away from us again."

In a mere half a second, she had lost her trusted partner of over ten years at the *Askeri İnzibat*. She expected the tears to fall freely, but she was still too shocked to cry. Everything had happened so quickly, she hadn't even had time to react.

What had gone wrong? Why hadn't she been able to anticipate the robot's move sooner? It was incredibly fast, but that was no excuse. She cursed herself silently, over and over again. There would be no forgiving herself for this.

"Yes, ma'am," Mataraci murmured, switching on his walkie-talkie.

Uzun, a tall, broad officer with light brown eyes, gave Demirci a pitying look. "Don't blame yourself," he said. "There was nothing we could have done in time to save him."

Demirci curled her lip and spat, "I don't need to hear *anything* from either of you right now until we get this situation under control."

Uzun nodded and fell silent, his caramel-colored eyes meeting the floor.

Demirci stood up and uneasily leaned a hand on Uzun's tricep for support. She was too short to reach up to his shoulder.

She had to call Lieutenant Ağa and let him know Azar was alive and unharmed.

What had Azar said to her? *"I'm making good progress with it."* What did that even mean? This thing was a machine programmed to hunt and destroy. Was it capable of brainwashing as well?

Mataraci clicked the radio back off and stepped forward to face Demirci. "We have officers on the way now," he said gently. "They're going to come pick up Rahmi *bey* and search the area for where they might have gone next. Let's get you home to rest."

Demirci shook her head firmly, casting a grim shadow over her face with a frown. "I am not resting until we hunt that thing down and capture it. Azar deserves a thorough interrogation as well. There is no time right now to rest."

Mataraci glanced hesitantly at Uzun. Both the officers knew there was no arguing with her.

"Let me make a phone call," Demirci grumbled, finally unlatching herself from Uzun's arm. She pulled her cell phone from her pocket and slowly walked down the street.

LIEUTENANT AĞA WAS charging down the steps of *Beylerbeyi Sarayı* when his phone began buzzing in his pocket. Cursing, he pulled it out with his right hand and looked at the screen. He didn't recognize the number calling. Ceylan, Topuz, and Parlak screeched to a halt behind the lieutenant just before nearly toppling him down the steps like a domino.

"Ağa," he wheezed, already out of breath from his speedy descent down the palace's massive stairwell.

"How's your arm, Lieutenant?"

Demirci's voice cut through the line like a shard of glass.

"It's been better," he grunted in response. "Luckily for me, Jamaković was there to diffuse the situation when the doctor told me I'd need to wait weeks for it to heal. I'm, uh...I'm still in the hospital." He ignored the bewildered looks darting from his colleagues' eyes.

Silence met him from the other end of the telephone. For a second, he thought the call had dropped. "Demirci? Hello?"

"Officer Jamaković is dead," came Demirci's sudden response. "The robot gutted him before we had a chance to react."

"W-what?" Ağa stammered, eyes widening and meeting the gaze of his three team members, who were all staring down from the step above him. "What do you mean?"

"I mean exactly what I just said," she snapped. "We found the robot hiding with Azar in a cemetery over in Üsküdar. It attacked out of nowhere."

Ağa could feel his blood pressure increasing. He feared they had already captured the robot and were back on their way to the military base with it.

"Azar was with the robot? Is she okay?" he asked.

"Oh, she's alright," Demirci said. "She's completely unharmed. In fact, she feels like she's made a certain progress with the robot. I don't have a clue what that means. Has she mentioned anything like that to you before?"

Ağa paused. Was Demirci coming to him for help?

"No," he said quickly. "I have no idea what that means. Did you capture the robot? What happened after it attacked?"

Out of the corner of his eye, Ağa could see Ceylan's eyes grow wide with anticipation. Parlak exchanged a nervous glance with Topuz.

"They're still on the run. We had no choice but to retreat after it attacked." Demirci sighed. "It's stronger than we anticipated. The bullets did absolutely nothing to harm its outer shell. We're significantly outgunned."

A flood of both joy and dread washed through Ağa's body upon hearing this. On the one hand, he was relieved that the robot had evaded the *Askeri İnzibat*'s grasp — and that Azar was still alive. On the other hand, he wondered at what he and his officers could possibly do should they have the chance to confront the robot. Their weapons were nowhere nearly as powerful as those that Demirci and her team carried. How was he supposed to incapacitate the thing with nothing more than a tiny handgun?

"Do you know where they went?" Ağa asked.

"No idea," Demirci said. "Chances are they left the cemetery as soon as we did. I wanted to give you a status update. Rest until your arm heals up. If Azar contacts you at all, please make sure that I'm the first to know about it."

The call ended with a click.

Ağa stared back up at his team.

"Well? What happened?" Topuz demanded.

Ağa shook his head. "We need to get a hold of Azar. They haven't captured it yet." He firmed up his tone and looked every officer in front of him straight in the eyes. "Istanbul is at a huge risk with this thing on the loose — but it's at an even bigger threat if Demirci and her team capture it before we do. Let's move."

Chapter Twenty-Eight

August 20, 2017

The sun was starting to set when Azar finally put her foot down.

"Stop," she gasped, struggling to speak against the winds that ripped across her face as Manti carried her through alleys and behind buildings at breakneck speed. The robot rounded a corner and stopped behind a dumpster. Azar fell from its arms.

"Is there a problem?" Manti quipped. It snapped down into compact form on all fours. Azar crouched next to it.

"Yes. I'm starving," she responded. "I need to find food. And a phone charger, before we get up to Sultançiftliği Taşlıtepe. Can you wait here and stay hidden? I won't be gone long." She really didn't like the idea of leaving the robot unsupervised, but her hunger and thirst were becoming too unbearable to keep ignoring them. She and Manti were making their way to a state forest in the mountains behind the city, and she didn't want to be without provisions before heading up.

"Yes," the robot replied. "I will stay here."

"Okay. Don't move. And *do not* hunt anyone else," she added, unsure of whether the robot would really adhere to her request or ignore her like it did the last time.

Azar walked out into the main street and suddenly became extremely self-conscious. She must have looked terrible. After getting only a few hours of sleep in the cold basement of a historic palace and spending the day crying and running like the wind, she was afraid to look at her own reflection passing in the windows of parked cars.

She stopped at the first kebab place she could find and ordered a lamb *döner*. Azar was grateful her wallet and phone had survived the journey thus far; she'd continuously checked the pockets of her zip-up to make sure they were still with her.

The cashier reluctantly handed her his iPhone charger after she practically begged his permission to borrow it. She thanked him and found a table near the wall to plug in her phone. She had to call the police station to make sure Ağa was okay.

As soon as the lamb *döner* was placed on her table, Azar scarfed it down immediately, unbothered by the looks she was getting from the table of college-aged girls across the restaurant. She cracked open the plastic water bottle and took three long swigs before looking back down at her phone. It was just starting to come back to life. She Googled the number for the Beşiktaş Police Station.

The receptionist told her that Ağa was currently out on business. Azar breathed a sigh of relief.

"So, he's okay?" she asked. "Is he injured?"

"Yes, he's doing fine," the receptionist replied. "He was here a few hours ago with a bandage around his arm, but other than that, everything seemed okay. He was bitten by a German Shepherd during one of his rounds."

Azar sank back in her chair, her shoulders relaxing and dropping down from her ears. Her outlook on the situation was much brighter now that she had received some food and some good news.

"Is there a personal line I can reach him at?" she asked, hoping the receptionist would be receptive to her request.

"Who am I speaking with? We usually don't give out officers' personal numbers for security reasons," said the receptionist.

"Azar Şamdereli," Azar responded. "Lieutenant Ağa was working on my father's case."

"Oh," she said, her voice sad and sincere. "Of course. Yes. Here's his number."

Azar typed the number into her notes app and thanked the receptionist. She hung up and then dialed Ağa right away, picking up the last shreds of cabbage and little crumbs of bread from the plate between her thumb and index finger. She debated ordering a second *döner.*

"Ağa," grunted Ağa on the other line.

"Lieutenant!" Azar was elated at hearing his voice, crystal clear through the phone. "It's Azar."

She heard an audible gasp on the other line. "Azar," he whispered. She could hear muffled voices in the background. "Are you okay? What's happening?"

"I-I just, I needed to buy time, so I decided to run with it. I have to figure out what this thing really is," she responded, nervously looking around the restaurant for any *Askeri İnzibat* officers that may have followed their trail. "I'm okay. It doesn't seem like it wants to harm me. But I need to figure out why before you capture it."

"Azar, listen to me," said Ağa. "Whatever you do, you *cannot* let the *Askeri İnzibat* find you. Do you understand? This robot was created for purposes that go a little beyond just national security."

Azar paused. "What do you mean? Wasn't it created as some sort of...military weapon?"

"Yes," Ağa hissed, "a weapon of war. But not war against adversaries abroad. War in Turkey. War against *civilians*." He spat out the last word, the contempt in his voice practically oozing through the phone.

Azar didn't understand right away. Her father had worked on something that was intended to battle civilians? It didn't make sense.

"Azar, this robot was created for use in riot control," Ağa growled into the phone. "Erbakan's people. It can't get into the hands of the military police. I will *not* stand by and watch my people get slashed into ribbons because Erbakan is tired of people fighting for their rights on the streets. Do you understand?"

Azar was shocked into absolute silence. She wanted to cry, but by this point, her tear ducts felt dry and depleted.

"How is that possible?" she stammered, trying to keep her voice down despite her rising hysteria. "There's no way my father would have taken on a project like that if he had known that's what it was for. He was always an activist, he would always go to the protests—"

No longer able to keep her voice down, Azar snatched the phone charger from the wall and slammed it back onto the counter on her way out the door. It was getting darker. She and Manti needed to get up to the forest before night had completely fallen.

"I heard one of the military officers say it myself," Ağa said grimly. "I'm sorry, Azar."

A car blasted its horn, causing Azar to jump backwards. She had walked directly into the street. She forgot to look for oncoming traffic before crossing.

"What do we do?" she asked, holding up a hand and jogging out of the irritated driver's way.

"I'll need to find a way to contain it and bring it back to our station. Where are you now?"

"We're on our way to Sultançiftliği Taşlıtepe. There's a campground up there with a few cabins. Hopefully, we can find shelter at up there."

"Wow. You two travel fast," Ağa murmured. "Alright. My team and I will be there as quickly as possible. Stay out of sight from absolutely everybody, got it?"

Azar nodded, then looked at her phone screen. "My phone is at three percent. If you can't get a hold of me later, it's because it died."

Ağa mumbled something incoherent. Azar bit her lower lip and rounded the corner to the dumpster where Manti had dropped her off. The robot was still there, folded neatly into a square behind the trash bins.

"I'll see you then." Azar hung up the phone and looked at Manti curled up on the floor. "Come on, you. Let's get out of here."

Chapter Twenty-Nine

August 20, 2017

Sultançiftliği Taşlıtepe State Forest was serene.

Tall, narrow trees sprouted endlessly along the mountain's crested ridge. The air was cooler and mistier here — and more importantly, there was no sign of any other humans here this late in the day. The climb up the mountain had been a mildly treacherous one, as hoisting Azar this whole time had started to strain Manti's limbs. But they reached the top right as the sun had disappeared beneath the horizon, and it made Azar seem a little more at ease. It could still tell that she was troubled deeply, but it was unsure as to why.

The prickling sensation still occurred every once in a while — the familiar, soft pulse of an electric current that seemed to instill peace and tranquility into Manti's processing system. It grew stronger the closer Azar was.

"There's a campground at the top of this trail," Azar said, pointing up a narrow, dimly lit walkway lined with trees. "Hopefully it's not too busy at this time of the summer. Maybe I can have a bed to sleep in tonight."

Campground.

Click.

Manti felt the new word seep into its athenaeum and let Azar lead the way.

There was relatively little movement up on the mountain, save for the few birds rustling in the branches and the squirrels darting on the ground to their resting places for the night. Manti began to power down thirty percent of its audio-visual processor to save energy, some of the lenses on its face slowly whirring to a stop. There was little risk of running into danger here.

Azar led the robot to a clearing at the top of the trail. A small wooden house stood in the clearing, surrounded by signs warning visitors of bears and poisonous centipedes that lived in the forest. The porch light was on, but the rest of the house looked dark inside. Beyond the house, similar ones dotted the hillside among the trees.

"Find somewhere to hide on the side," Azar whispered to the robot once they neared the entrance. "If they're able to give me a cabin tonight, I'll let them show me to it and come back to get you. Otherwise, we'll figure something else out. Do you understand?"

"I compute."

Azar nodded and turned back to the entrance of the small cabin. Manti turned the corner towards the dark and indiscernible leaves of the forest.

The sound of human footsteps suddenly made themselves present in Manti's audio-visual processing system. The robot paused.

Somebody was coming around the side of the small building from the back.

Manti kicked itself into high gear and made a run for the trees. It tried to ignore the hunger tugging at its core. Its earlier kill had felt right, even though it had sent Azar into a tailspin.

Manti recalled the tears streaming down her face and worked harder to suppress the urge to unsheathe its claws.

From the cover of darkness, Manti could see the person who was rounding the corner. It was a woman wearing long sleeves, pants, and a navy blue covering on her head. Manti had seen many women wearing these types of coverings before but had never been able to find out what they were called. She was humming softly, almost nervously, to herself. She kept glancing over her shoulder as she walked.

As the woman got closer, Manti used a few of its visual lenses to zoom in for a closer look.

She looked oddly familiar.

Zooming closer in, the robot got a good look at the woman's face.

She seemed to be about in the middle of her life, perhaps in her late thirties. She wore big, round glasses that sat on top of her squishy-looking nose.

Manti had seen this woman before.

Almost involuntarily, as if propelled by some unseen force of nature, the robot lurched back out from the forest.

The woman blinked, shocked that something had appeared so quickly and so suddenly to obstruct her path. As soon as she realized what was standing in front of her, she let out a horrifying scream.

Chapter Thirty

August 20, 2017

Azar knocked on the door of the ranger's cabin three times, but to no avail. They had likely gotten to the campsite just a hair too late to find shelter for tonight.

The bloodcurdling scream ripped through the trees just as Azar was turning back around to think of a plan B. Goosebumps rattled her arms. Had Manti been unable to suppress its bloodlust once again?

Azar took off running down the wooden steps of the cabin in the direction of the scream. It sounded like whoever had uttered it was close by. Perhaps she could get there in time to coax Manti away and to stop the victim's bleeding.

Rounding the corner to the side of the house, Azar saw Manti standing in front of her, its figure looming over a person she couldn't make out clearly.

"Stop!" she yelled, praying that she wasn't running directly into another massacre. She skidded to a halt next to Manti and looked at the woman standing in front of her.

She seemed completely unharmed, besides the fact that she looked terrified out of her mind. She was wearing a dark blue *hijab* and thick round glasses over her bulging eyes. Azar whispered a silent prayer of thanks that she had been able to get there before Manti tore into the woman's abdomen.

"Are you okay?" Azar asked, panting from her short burst down the stairs and around the corner of the cabin. "It's not going to hurt you." She paused and stared. Somehow, she recognized this woman, but the feeling was distant. It reminded Azar of remembering a song's lyrics but being unable to conjure the melody in her head. Where had she seen this woman before?

"*Aman allahım*," the woman whispered, taking a step back and putting a trembling hand to her face. She looked at Azar, then at the robot, then back to Azar again. "Are you — are you Azar Şamdereli?"

It was Azar's turn to stare, too stunned to speak.

The woman took another step back. "What are you doing here?" she asked. "Please don't — how did you find me?" It was clear that she knew exactly what this robot was capable of and feared for her life.

"Find you?" Azar echoed, stuttering, unsure of how to formulate her next sentence. "What — we didn't find you, I just — how — who are you?"

The woman gave Azar and Manti a long, hard stare-down before speaking again.

"My name is Çakır Müjde," she finally responded, her voice coming slowly and deliberately as she looked at the ground. "I was part of the research team that created the robot next to you. I worked closely with your father." At this, she adjusted her glasses, still keeping her gaze rooted firmly by her feet.

Azar almost doubled over in shock. Her mind raced back to just the day before, when she had barged into the office door and discovered that Müjde had disappeared. Papers littering the desk and the floor were the only things she had left behind.

She realized now that the reason she recognized the professor's face was because her headshot was hung up on her office door, next to her nameplate.

Had the professor fled to the top of the mountain after Mustafa had been discovered dead?

"You left the university," Azar said. "I went to go find you there, but you were already gone."

Müjde looked up again. Tears welled behind her big, round glasses.

"Yes," she responded meekly. It looked like she was going to say something else, but she just lowered her gaze to the ground again.

"What happened?" Azar asked, a wave of elation rising in her chest. This was exactly what she needed. It was another chance at finding the answers she needed.

"Did you know I was here?" the professor asked again. "I promise, I'll tell you whatever you need to know. But please, don't let it hurt me." She looked back up at Manti, despair swimming in her eyes.

Azar suddenly realized that the professor thought she and Manti had hunted her down.

"No, no. Don't worry." She took a step toward the trembling Müjde. The professor flinched and stepped back. Azar paused. "We came here to look for a cabin for the night. The *Askeri İnzibat* are hunting us down. Lieutenant Ağa and his team should be on their way up here as we speak to help us. Everything is going to be okay," she added softly when she realized tears had begun trickling down Müjde's face.

"The *Askeri İnzibat*?" Müjde's eyes widened as her head snapped back up. She took her glasses off and rubbed the tears from her cheeks, her tone now urgent. "That's not good."

"I agree," Azar said grimly. "Can you help us find shelter until Ağa gets here?"

Müjde hesitated but finally nodded, her eyes darting toward Manti. "Is it going to be safe?"

Azar mustered a close-lipped smile. "We'll see," she answered truthfully, "but we can't just keep sitting out here like live bait. The police have tracking devices and guns. Very big machine guns. We need to hide as quickly as we can."

Müjde nodded in understanding. She returned Azar's sad, sullen smile.

"Follow me."

OFFICER DEMIRCI CLICKED her phone off and reached for her walkie-talkie. Dusk was rapidly approaching. They needed to get up to the mountain as soon as they could.

Ağa should have known better than to accept a call on his cell phone. A simple wiretap app made it a breeze for Demirci to listen to all of his personal conversations.

"Mataraci. Get the car," she barked into the radio, a subtle grin pulling at the corners of her mouth. "We're taking a trip up to the mountain tonight."

Chapter Thirty-One

August 20, 2017

Professor Müjde's cabin was on the opposite end of the grounds. Azar and Manti followed her there in absolute silence. No matter how tranquil the robot seemed, Azar couldn't shake the small flame of fear flickering in her heart that it might attack at any moment.

Müjde made two cups of tea upon entering the small, rickety cabin. It was only one room with a small kitchen, a dresser, and a double bed in the middle of the hardwood floor. Azar realized that the bathrooms were outhouses down the path—the likely reason why they had run into Müjde so far from her cabin just as night was falling. She shivered, crossing her arms tightly over her chest.

"You can have a blanket if you're cold," Müjde said, handing her the cup of tea and beckoning for her to take a seat at the tiny round table near the stove. "I know it gets chillier up here than it does in the city."

Azar thanked her and took up the offer, wrapping herself in a thick quilt Müjde pulled out from the dresser and blowing on the cup of tea.

Manti clicked back down onto all fours and rested silently at the threshold of the door, eyes whirring.

Müjde looked uneasily at the robot and sat down across from Azar at the table. Now that Azar was able to look at her in the light, she noticed that the professor seemed to just have a permanently sad look on her face. Her expression rarely changed as she talked.

"Azar, I'm so sorry about what happened to your father," Müjde said, her voice threatening to break. Azar felt tears prick at the backs of her eyes.

"Thanks," she mumbled, taking a sip of the scalding tea to avoid having to say anything else.

"I know you must be extremely angry with me," Müjde continued, the same worried look etched onto her face, "and the rest of us. I'm sure you have questions. I just want to start out by saying that we had absolutely no idea that it was going to turn to this."

"I'm sure you didn't," Azar said dryly. "But everything happened. And here we are. So, let me ask you — why did you take on a project that would be used against civilians during protests and riots?"

Müjde looked like someone slapped her in the face and began shaking her head violently, in quick little bursts. "No, no, no," she stammered briskly. "We didn't know."

Azar furrowed her brow at the professor. "What do you mean, you didn't know?"

"We weren't told initially what its intended use was," Müjde replied. "We were told that it was an experiment only for use in national emergencies and security purposes. We didn't find out what we *really* were creating this for until much later. That's when all the trouble began."

"What trouble?" Azar pulled the blanket in tighter to her body. "You mean, my father getting ripped into pieces by his own creation, or?"

Müjde's mouth became a thin straight line. "No...well, kind of. It led up to that. Had your father not done what he did...well." She looked down at her cup of tea and sighed. "It may have never happened if he wasn't there when he was."

Azar raised an eyebrow. "What do you mean, 'what he did?'"

Müjde met Azar's steely glare with eyes big and round like a calf's. "Azar," she said softly. "Your father had been conducting a procedure on the robot during its final stages of DNA transference in secret. For months. I only found out by accident, when I found him in the laboratory late one night on my way home."

Azar couldn't keep her jaw from dropping wide open. "What? W-what does that mean?"

"When I walked in there that night," Müjde said, looking pained, "he was sitting in the chair next to the lifegiving chamber—what we used to inject the robot with its necessary lifefluid — bent over almost halfway. At first, I thought he was asleep, but when he looked up at me, I saw that he had something in his arm. It was a tube. And then...it was difficult for me to realize what was going on at first because it was all so strange...but then I realized that he was hooked up to the chamber through an IV tube in his arm. Azar, he'd been feeding the robot from his own body for months."

Azar sat in shocked silence at the table. Neither of the two women moved.

"Feeding it?" Azar whispered shakily, finally getting a grasp of her own voice again. "Feeding it how?"

"The robot was created to be a perfect hybrid between a living thing and a machine," Müjde said. "We designed it to contain a synthetic circulatory system — similar to that of humans — that acts like somewhat of a nervous system. It pumps a vital fluid through its body and send signals to its central processing unit as to how it should behave. It was the most effective way to ensure the robot would behave just like a natural predator would without question. We allowed it to feel hunger, a primal instinct that would never fail to drive the robot's ability and will to attack people. Unfortunately, we weren't able to advance far enough into the experiment to set controls on the robot's hunger before it managed to escape." Müjde's eyes were sad and tired behind her thick round lenses.

"Not only that, but should anyone ever decide they needed the robot for other uses, the fluid could be easily drained and replaced, giving it other characteristics that might be better for a different scenario. For this first experiment, took DNA from a lion, given that it's the most powerful predator on land with amazing stalking and hunting techniques. It also possesses a pack mentality, meaning that had we been able to create more of these things, it would have been naturally in sync with them. But the robot could be easily infused with the DNA from a shark, for example, should there be a need for its abilities in marine warfare."

Azar drank the information in like someone who had just had their first taste of water after days lost in the desert. So, her guess about the robot's genetic makeup *had* been correct.

"Pack mentality," she repeated. "That's why...that's why it could sense when I was in danger. It was as if I was a part of its pack."

"Once we discovered the true purpose of these machines," Müjde continued, "the department head called a meeting to discuss the importance of keeping the mission top secret on behalf of the government. Your father was the only one to speak out. He found it monstrous that we, especially as scientists and educators, would involve ourselves with something that intended to hurt or even kill civilians. It got intense," she added, a small smile creeping onto her face. "He was very visibly upset but bound to secrecy. He decided to take matters into his own hands."

Azar could barely hear the whirring noise that was coming from Manti's eyes spinning behind her. Everything sounded distant and foreign in her ears.

"When I stumbled in on him that night, I thought he had maybe been injured, but he was able to speak to me. I swore I wouldn't tell anyone...no one else knows, I promise. He was adding his own DNA into the mix because he couldn't stand the thought of giving a robot purely killer instincts without any sort of counterbalance. It was incredibly risky, as nothing like this has ever been attempted, as far as we know."

Müjde leaned over the table and stared deeply into Azar's eyes.

"He did it so the robot could possess the rationality and empathy so unique to human beings," she whispered gently. "He was trying to protect us."

Azar felt a giant, searing hole tearing through her heart and across her entire chest. It burned so painfully that she dropped her chin to her collarbones and let out a sob.

"That's...that's why," she finally managed, sniffling softly. She turned back to Manti, who was still folded perfectly on the ground at the door. "The robot...it won't hunt me. It could even sense when I was in danger or sad. It's been trying to protect me this whole time."

Müjde's frown deepened even further than Azar thought was possible, the corners of her big eyes drooping behind her thick round glasses.

Azar looked back up at the professor. "He was getting so frail and weak towards the end," she continued, wiping her nose on the edge of the quilt.

"Yes. He was losing a lot of blood, day in and day out, extracting DNA to add into the fluid," Müjde responded. "I wish it would have been as easy as a simple cheek swab, but unfortunately, that doesn't yield the same caliber of DNA that blood sampling does."

Azar felt dizzy. She took another sip of tea to try and calm her system.

"The robot likely would have escaped regardless." Müjde sighed. "Unfortunately, it was becoming conscious — and *strong* — at a faster rate than we had anticipated. We never expected it would gain such an inquisitive consciousness like it did, but that likely had to do with the human DNA it was feeding on. At any rate, had Mustafa not been in the lab so late, it may not have attacked him that night."

The professor leaned back into her chair again, nervously adjusting her glasses. "I've been up here since Monday," she admitted. "I was so afraid. I thought maybe it was hunting — and if it recognized me somewhere, it would attack. But even more so, I just feel awful guilt." She gave Azar a sad half-smile. "The rest of us just followed orders and tried not to think what might happen if we made this experiment a reality. But he did something about it. And he died because of it. He died trying to do something for the good of the people of Istanbul."

Azar looked back at Manti, holding back tears. "Well. He didn't die completely, did he?"

Müjde's sad smile suddenly vanished. She stood up, craning her neck to the door. "Do you hear that?" she asked in a panicked whisper. "I hear footsteps outside."

"It's probably Ağa," Azar said, standing up and leaning over to look out the window by the table. She checked her phone. It had died again. Her heart thumped unevenly against her ribs.

"We can't take any chances," Müjde murmured. "Close the curtain. We need to hide the robot."

Manti had clicked back up onto its two limbs. The lenses on its face were spinning in faster circles. Azar felt a fresh influx of anxiety take hold of her nerves. Whenever Manti looked alert like that, the outcome was never good.

"There is danger approaching," it said suddenly.

"*Aman allahım,* so it does talk," Müjde said softly. A genuine smile broke out across her face. "Incredible."

"I believe what it's saying," Azar said grimly. She scanned the room. "Manti, can you fit under the bed?"

Müjde shot her an inquisitive look. "You named the robot?"

"It was...an interrogation tactic," Azar huffed, blushing. "It just stuck."

In response, Manti snapped back down onto all fours and scuttled under the bed like a crab.

A heavy knock pounded on the cabin door.

"*Askeri İnzibat*," came Demirci's voice from outside, icy cold and sharp. "Open the door. Now."

Chapter Thirty-Two

August 20, 2017

Azar looked into Müjde's eyes, frantic. The professor looked like she had just been told a devastating piece of news but gave Azar a firm nod. Reluctantly, Azar reached over and opened the door.

Demirci was standing in front of her, arms crossed, the two other officers behind her. A pain pierced Azar's heart at noticing Jamaković's absence.

"Where is it?" Demirci snapped, machine gun pointed directly at the spot in between Azar's eyebrows.

"I...I don't know," Azar stammered. She took a deep breath in and exhaled loudly. "After the cemetery, I was so scared. I ran away from it. I don't know where it went."

Demirci gave Azar a deadpan expression. "Interesting." She chuckled. "Then why are our trackers pointing us directly behind where you're standing?"

Azar squeezed her eyes shut. In her panic, she had momentarily forgotten about the stupid tracking devices. Red dots swam like little amoebas on the inside of her eyelids.

"We will not surrender it to you," Müjde stepped in, her voice suddenly firm and authoritative. She sounded nothing like the meek, scared woman from a couple seconds ago.

"I'm going to give you three seconds to let us in before we forcibly enter," Demirci growled. "And trust me, you don't want us to reach that point."

Out of the darkness in the trees behind the military officers, the sound of a gun clicking emerged. Azar couldn't see beyond Officer Mataraci, but she saw him gasp and his eyes grow round.

"What...?"

Demirci turned around just as Lieutenant Ağa stepped out of the shadows, the nose of his handgun planted firmly on Mataraci's temple. He was flanked by three of his own officers, also brandishing guns. They looked like toys compared to the *Askeri İnzibat*'s terrifying weapons.

"We'll take it from here, Demirci," Ağa rumbled.

Ceylan stepped up to Demirci and cocked his gun to her head as well. Topuz stood with his to Uzun. An officer Azar hadn't seen before stepped in front of her and Müjde and faced the *Askeri İnzibat*, her own pistol drawn. Azar couldn't help but stare at Ağa's makeshift sling and bloodstained bandage covering his entire arm.

Demirci looked momentarily taken aback and then visibly frustrated. "Ağa," she snarled, "don't try to play this game with me. It's not worth it for you."

"Oh, I think it will be very worth it." Ağa was very clearly trying to muster as much strength into his voice as possible, but Azar noticed a slight wince. She could only guess how much pain must have been coursing through his bandaged, tattered arm.

"I'm going to make this really simple," Demirci said coolly. "I'm going to go inside the cabin and find out where the robot is hiding. My officers and I are going to leave with said robot. Once we do that, you all will be free to go and can go on with your lives, pretending like none of this ever happened." Inwardly, Azar marveled at her calm, collected demeanor. She'd clearly had a gun held to her head numerous times before this one.

"We can't let you take it," Azar blurted. "We know what it's going to be used for. How dare you create a weapon like this for use on innocent civilians?"

"I'm not here to stand on your moral high ground, Azar," Demirci said, venom in her voice. "I'm here to serve my government and to keep the peace. Let me inside or I'm ordering my officers to fire."

"That's not going to work out well for you, Demirci," Ağa growled, giving his gun a little bump against Mataraci's temple. The young officer winced. Demirci went deadly silent.

Her next move was so swift that Azar could hardly think to scream.

With a graceful pivot, Demirci whipped around to face Ceylan, who was still holding the gun to her temple. Before he had time to react, the *Askeri İnzibat* officer slammed the butt of her massive weapon to his forehead. Ceylan crumpled to the floor with a sickening crunch. Azar felt her vision start to blur.

The officer standing in front Azar let out a bellow and cocked her handgun, but Demirci was faster than she was. Demirci lunged, thrusting her gun into the officer's midsection. The officer howled in pain, doubling over the weapon pressed to her stomach. Demirci yanked her arms to the right, flinging the officer off to the side. She advanced toward Azar with intense velocity, lifting her weapon like a wasp poised to sting. Azar felt the cool metal of the gun's muzzle pressing firmly into her forehead. Every muscle in her body froze. A cold sweat prickled at the back of her neck and her stomach began to churn.

"One move from either of you, and I won't hesitate to fire," Demirci barked at Ağa, who was bent over Ceylan's unconscious body, and the other officer, who was wobbling back up on her feet. Demirci turned her icy gaze back to Azar.

"Listen to me, Azar," she hissed, her voice cool and collected as it slithered from behind her clenched teeth. "This is not a game. Your stupidity is costing us dearly. Officer Jamaković is dead because of you."

Azar felt the officer's words slice like daggers into her skin, but she didn't lower her gaze. Though Demirci's face was calm and stoic, her eyes were wild with unhinged fury.

"I have already lost far too much," Demirci continued. For a brief moment, Azar thought she heard the officer's voice quiver ever so slightly. "I will not return from this mission with nothing to show for my struggle. Do you understand me?"

Azar said nothing. She bored holes into Demirci's eyes, trying to ignore the rising tide of nausea building in her stomach. She heard Müjde utter something next to her, but it was incomprehensible.

Somewhere in the trees above them, an owl crooned.

"Azar!" Müjde's voice finally rang clear in Azar's ears. Demirci had taken a step back and removed the gun from her forehead. Azar turned to face Müjde and stifled a scream.

Manti was standing at her shoulder, claws unsheathed.

Azar found her voice at last. "Manti, don't —"

She could hardly speak. Terror gripped her throat as she watched the robot stalk toward Demirci. Uzun and Mataraci ran to flank her sides, weapons drawn, as the robot advanced.

It was clear that Manti was hesitating. Azar could tell its movements were calculated, almost as if they weren't being driven by its primordial hunger, but rather by another governing force: conscious decision-making.

"Manti, please don't." Azar tried again, this time mustering as much strength as she could and pushing it out through her voice. "No more. It's not worth it. Please."

The robot paused.

Despite the chilliness of the mountain air, Azar was sweating bullets. Her pulse was racing as aggressively as a bull in a china store. She looked over at Müjde again, whose sad eyes stared bleakly in horror at what was about to unfold. Manti lifted its claws and took another step toward Demirci. Azar squeezed her eyes shut, unable to watch another bloodbath.

"I sense your anguish when I kill," the robot chirped, turning its head around to face Azar.

Azar's eyes snapped back open. Demirci's eyebrows shot up her forehead in surprise.

"I was created to hunt," it continued, "and that causes you pain." Manti's eyes were twisting their slow, sad, deliberate circles on its face, clicking and whirring.

Stunned, Ağa began to slowly lift himself from his crouch at Ceylan's head. Demirci's steely stare didn't waver and neither did her arms holding up the massive gun in front of her.

"Yes," Azar whispered, tears threatening to sting at her eyes. "that's correct."

"I sense that I am the cause of your pain," Manti replied. "I will cause no more suffering for you, Azar." Slowly, the robot drew its claws back toward itself.

Demirci gasped. She stepped forward and pressed the gun against the robot's trunk. "No rash moves. Your creator commands it. Do not disengage. You are coming with us."

Manti's eyes were still fixated on Azar, twisting and turning. It seemed unbothered by Demirci's weapon on its body. Azar returned the stare, unable to move, suddenly feeling like an anvil had been placed onto her chest.

She realized she was losing the only piece of her father she had left.

"It's going to destroy itself for you, Azar," Müjde whispered, trembling.

It happened in an instant, almost too quickly for human eyes to see. Azar let out a shriek as the robot drew its claws through its midsection, slicing its metal casing open with a gut-wrenching screech and falling to the floor in pieces.

Chapter Thirty-Three

August 22, 2017

The drive to Hayriye from Istanbul's Beşiktaş neighborhood took about three hours. Azar sat in the front seat of Ediz's little green Opel, gently but firmly cradling the ornate gold and turquoise urn on her lap, her head bobbing to the sound of Ibrahim Tatlises serenading softly on the radio. The winding roads up to Hayriye always used to make Azar carsick when she was younger, but now, watching the rolling green hills rush by her in the window, she felt stronger. Her stomach had unclenched itself from the tight and unforgiving knot it had been consistently wrapped in over the last week.

Ediz pulled into a turnout along the highway and turned the ignition off. She turned to Azar and to Ömer, who was sitting in the backseat. "Are you two ready?"

The siblings nodded. Azar unbuckled her seat belt and opened the door, making sure to be careful with the urn carrying her father's ashes as she stepped from the car. She walked to the edge of the hillside and looked at the sprawling village in the valley below. A strong wind picked up her thick black hair and wrapped it around her face with a whoosh.

Everything looked so small from up above. The rooftops were mere red dots on the endless green canvas of the hills; the roads snaking through the village were like worms sprouting from the earth after fresh rainfall. Wildflowers dotted the hills like pink and yellow chalk dust. From here, everything seemed distant and obsolete. The events of the last few days seemed like a long ago past to Azar.

AFTER MANTI RIPPED itself apart, the group of shellshocked humans stood in stunned silence around its broken body, its two halves oozing with its green lifefluid and shooting sparks from its frayed wires.

Müjde was the first to speak.

"This...this was never in the plan," she said, looking up at the horrified police officers in front of her, still frozen with their weapons drawn. "We never programmed it for self-destruction. Nor...guilt." She shot Azar a quick side-eye glance before continuing. "I don't know what happened. This shouldn't have been possible."

Demirci wordlessly turned on her heel and stormed away, her two flabbergasted companions close behind her. By then, Ceylan had come to and stared at the wreckage around him in stunned silence. Azar and Müjde picked up the pieces of the robot and gotten a ride back into Istanbul with Lieutenant Ağa while the rest of the officers took a separate car back to the station.

"Thank you for everything, Lieutenant," Azar said. The shock was beginning to wear off, the numbness leaving her body and being replaced with overwhelming sadness and exhaustion. "I don't know how we would have survived that one without you."

"You did well, Azar," Ağa murmured. "We're lucky you were so headstrong. We would have been in big trouble had you just handed the machine over to them."

Azar looked at her reflection in the window. Dark half-moons circled underneath her eyes, and her long hair was wind-swept and matted.

"It must have been terrifying," Müjde said from the back seat, "running with it, never knowing what was going to happen next. It could have killed you easily, for all you knew."

Azar looked back from the window. "Yeah," she said with a sad smile. "It was. But it was also one of the most amazing experiences of my life so far. It was like I got to spend a little extra time with my dad after he died before he completely vanished, like he was telling me the whole time that I should trust my gut and that everything was going to be okay."

"What are you going to do with the pieces?" Ağa asked, turning to Müjde in the backseat.

"I think the robotics team at the university will be happy to recycle what they can from the body," she said, running a finger smoothly over the robot's still-exposed claws sitting on her lap. They were caked with dried green fluid and flecks of blood from its earlier kill. "Or perhaps I should just put it on the department head's desk as a gift."

"If you don't mind, I'd like to take a piece back to the station with me. If my team can run proper tests on it, we'll be able to easily recognize this kind of technology, should anyone ever try to do something like this again in the future," Ağa said.

"I think that's a good idea," Müjde replied. "We have no idea what the *Askeri İnzibat* is going to try and conjure up next."

"We'll keep a good eye on them," Ağa growled. "I need some peace and quiet after these last couple of months. If they try and pull any more stunts like this, I'm going to lose my mind."

Azar could hardly keep her eyes open as she watched the trees of the state forest rush by her.

NOW, STANDING NEXT to the Opel up in the winding slopes of Hayriye, Azar felt at peace. All that mattered in this moment was the task at hand: to set Mustafa's ashes free from their ceramic confinement.

As the three stood at the top of the hill, Ediz looked at her daughter, staring wordlessly into the distance, her black hair whipping through the wind like a flag on a ship.

"Do you want to begin?" she asked softly.

Azar sighed and nodded. Slowly, she removed the lid from the urn.

"This is for the man who made the ultimate sacrifice for his people," Azar said, her long face stoic and calm, the soft gray powder beginning to trickle out of the urn and take flight in the wind. Despite the sadness seeping into her heart, her voice was calm and clear.

"This is for standing up for what is right and for sometimes needing to trust in the waves to pull you in the right direction. Even if it feels like you might be drowning." Azar looked up at the endless azure sky, letting her skin drink in the rays of sun and basking in their warmth. "Even if it feels like you have no idea if you can pull yourself to shore."

The last few particles of ash trickled out from the urn and disappeared off the hillside in the breath of the wind.

About the Author

Cecilia Seiter is a freelance writer, author, and poet. She is based in Los Angeles but is often found in the other cities she calls home: Berlin, Germany and Oakland, California. Her work has received accolades from the UC Berkeley School of Journalism and the California College Media Association. Man Made Hunter is her debut novel.

About the Publisher

LM Vintage Publishers

We are a traditional, royalty paying publisher with a unique approach.

A proud member of the Independent Book Publishers Association.

www.lmvintagepublishers.com